DANNY MALLOY
Samurai Summer

Books also published by M. A. Hugger

**Danny Malloy and His
Mississippi River Samurai**

DANNY MALLOY
Samurai Summer

M. A. Hugger

iUniverse, Inc.
New York   Bloomington

Danny Malloy, Samurai Summer

Copyright © 2010 M. A. Hugger

This is a work of fiction. All of the characters, names, incidents, organizations, and dialogue in this novel are either the products of the author's imagination or are used fictitiously.

iUniverse books may be ordered through booksellers or by contacting:

iUniverse
1663 Liberty Drive
Bloomington, IN 47403
www.iuniverse.com
1-800-Authors (1-800-288-4677)

Because of the dynamic nature of the Internet, any Web addresses or links contained in this book may have changed since publication and may no longer be valid. The views expressed in this work are solely those of the author and do not necessarily reflect the views of the publisher, and the publisher hereby disclaims any responsibility for them.

ISBN: 978-1-4502-6402-0 (pbk)
ISBN: 978-1-4502-6404-4 (cloth)
ISBN: 978-1-4502-6403-7 (ebk)

Printed in the United States of America

iUniverse rev. date: 11/12/2010

Security is mostly a superstition.

Helen Keller from The Open Door (1957)

Acknowledgements

Special thanks to those who have encouraged me to tell this Danny story: Keith Larson, Peggy Backup, Nicole Borg, Anne Berry, Dennis Schwesinger, Katy Kickman, Lillian Kruger and students from Kellogg MN's River Valley Academy.
M.A. Hugger

DANNY MALLOY'S SAMURAI SUMMER WORLD

DRAGON COURAGE

"YOU'RE CHANGIN' EVERYTHIN'!" Danny screams into the phone. "You never tell me nothin'!" He slams down the receiver and pounds the wall. He stomps his feet. He'd kick the baseboard if Mr. Nowell, his foster dad, wasn't watching.

"No vacation! I ain't goin' home." Danny holds his stomach as if he's been hit in the gut by a fist instead of words. His vacation is off. Jenny, his probation officer, says his mother has lost her job at Joe's Bar and plans to go back to school. No vacation, but he can visit his mom this weekend and help her move. Jenny has arranged it. She'll pick him up on Saturday.

He feels Mrs. Nowell move toward him.

"You worked so hard to go home this summer," she says quietly, careful not to touch him.

All the bad words he knows burn on his lips. Mr. Nowell steps closer.

Run! Run! Run! The thoughts make his legs quiver. Hot tears well behind his eyelids, but he can't let the Nowells see him cry. He heads for his room, slams the door hard, throws himself on the bed, and kicks off his boots. He lies on his back and counts the ceiling tiles, though he knows there are a hundred ninety-six. He wipes his nose on the bedspread.

After his heart stops racing, Danny kneels at the window. His green dragon rests atop a bluff across the Mississippi River in Wisconsin, guarding the river's flyway. Danny brought the dragon from the Hamm Farm and School for Juveniles. Though the dragon is make-believe, the sight of the monster makes Danny feel safe. The dragon reminds Danny he's Samurai. And, like the ancient warriors who became the elite, he recites a haiku to capture his thoughts:

O Dragon Green
Give me courage, give me heart
Keep me Samurai

Danny moogles, or thinks, *my mother always causes trouble. What did she do to get fired? If she's not workin' for Joe's that means there ain't no job for me. And going to school? Her?* He snorts and scrunches his forehead into a frown. He flops on the bed, rolls over on his stomach and cups his cheeks in the palms of his hands. *Jenny says my mom is movin' and I can help. Big deal!*

His first move from home was to Hamm, through the system. The high school principal, a Mrs. George, turned him in for truancy, getting up late and skipping school. She reported him to the county social worker, a Mrs. Badge, who then called the cop, who ate salami. The cop arrested him a couple of times for violating curfew and for borrowing stuff: apples, soda, and pizza. The cop was a mumbler and grumbler, who made his mom cry. After the cop came the judge, a gray-haired old lady, who sat in a big office and pounded her fist on the desk. She sentenced him to Hamm, five years.

And my mom just sat there, dumb and stupid, as if she'd ever been there for me. I needed my dad. Danny wipes his eyes on his shirt sleeves and reaches under the mattress for a girly magazine. He flips the slick pages without seeing. His eyelids close. He's tired inside, too tired to make run-away plans. *Where to go? How to get there? Where to find money and food? Why is my life not fair? I need to go home, to a real home. This is my fifth foster home.* He drifts off knowing his sleep keeps the world out.

CROW MURDER

THE NEXT MORNING the sound of crows shrieking outside Danny's window through the gray mist, awaken him. His gut says the owl is in trouble, a young bird abandoned by its mother, like him, a foster kid.

Danny rolls out of his blanket nest, wipes his nose on his pajama sleeve and moves his tongue across his teeth. His mouth tastes, his body yearns for that first cigarette. He has sort'a given up smoking, stopped skipping school and does his homework, everything Jenny made him promise to do so he could go home for the summer. He wanted to go home, where he could sleep late, smoke, hang out at Joe's Bar and watch TV. At home he feels safe. Jenny's promise for the summer kept him from running away from the Nowells.

The crows sound again. He jerks up his jeans, elbows into a blue T-shirt that matches his eyes and pulls on his silver-toed cowboy boots. The boots once belonged to Mr. Nowell. Danny bought them with money he earned gathering mushrooms with his new friends, Walter and Anne Goulette. He never imagined earning three-hundred dollars or eating mushrooms.

The crows send up a new wave of shrieks as Danny swings his legs over the deck rail. The Nowells' house sits on a high bank that overlooks the river.

"Three miles across," Mr. Nowell said. "From here to Wisconsin, nothing but water and sky."

Danny heads down the path to the river between patches of purple vetch and clumps of orange, tiger-lilies. When it rains the path turns slippery.

Mr. Nowell waits where the path divides into two ways, one way goes to the river and the other to the owl's tree. The man stands over six feet tall, and has more middle now than shows in his Marine pictures.

"The ruckus woke you, too?" Mr. Nowell's black hair pokes out from under a cap that advertises Curly's Bait Shop. He wears a black and red checkered wool jacket.

Danny nods and hunches his shoulders.

Black crows circle the owl's tree. More crows sway in nearby tree tops. Their chants make the leaves quiver like heat rising from a road on a hot day.

"Our owl goofed," Mr. Nowell says, "stayed out too late. Crows followed him home and discovered his nest. His secret's out."

"Ain't he bigger than a crow?" Danny stomps his boots in the wet grass and shivers. *Wish I'd put on a sweatshirt*, he moogles.

"True, but one owl against a gang of crows makes for trouble. In fact, a gang of crows is called a *murder*."

"Will they kill him?"

"They could."

Danny shivers again. Mr. Nowell takes off his jacket and drapes it across Danny's shoulders. Quietly he points out the scene. "See the crows sitting high in those trees? They're the lookouts, they summoned the other crows. They make the cheering section and rev up the tension. The attackers are there." He points to branches nearer the owl's tree. "The crows' strategy is to make the owl *break cover*. If the owl stays and waits, the crows will give up and go away."

Then, I hope he's not like me, Danny moogles, *I'd break cover.*

More crows join the cheering section.

Mr. Nowell shakes his head. "If the owl flies, he's in trouble."

"What can we do?" Danny asks.

"Nothing," the man says. "Think good thoughts. It's up to the owl. If he stays put, he'll survive."

Danny watches the crows circle the tree. He imagines being the owl and does a haiku for the bird like Jenny says to do when he's scared or has to make a decision.

Hunker down young owl
You have blown your secret so
Stay. Don't break cover

Mr. Nowell turns and starts up the steep river path. Danny follows and covers his ears. The crows' caws beat time with the thumps in his heart.

Packing Up

Mid-morning Mrs. Nowell knocks and slowly opens Danny's door. "I threw away your Hamm box. Instead, use this for the weekend." She holds out a brown knapsack.

He came to the Nowells in March, three months ago, with all his possessions packed in a cardboard box. The girly magazines were under his mattress, but the blue-velvet, eagle jacket now hung in her closet. He found it one day while nosing around, casing the joint. He also found pictures of Mr. Nowell in a Marine uniform holding a golden saber and a young Mrs. Nowell with blond hair wearing a blue dress and white shoes.

Mrs. Nowell walks to his dresser, opens the top drawer, and pushes the contents around.

She's lookin' for cigarettes. Lady, when I had them, I hid them under the bottom drawer.

She mumbles and pushes her silver hair away from her face. Her arms are freckled with brown spots. She shakes open a T-shirt and a pair of undershorts. "Are you going to wear tennis shoes or your boots?"

"Boots, wanna show my mom." He remembers getting the boots:

On his first night at the river he followed Mr. Nowell down to the cove to feed the owl. The path was slippery and muddy and his Nikes were still wet the next morning. He didn't have shoes for school.

So he'd rented Mr. Nowell's silver-toed, cowboy boots with his seven dollars and the eagle jacket. The boots got him respect. The guys in his classes admired them, and the girls shared their pizza. Anne, Walter's sister, had even slipped him some smoke sticks for free. But later, when he returned the boots and asked for his money and the jacket back, Mr. Nowell said rent was not like buying something. When you rent, you don't keep what you rented, and you don't get your money back. The Nowells had kept his money and the jacket. Even when he earned the three-hundred dollars and bought the boots, the Nowells kept the jacket. He felt robbed.

"Get your stuff." Mrs. Nowell holds out the knapsack. Danny hands her a comb, a toothbrush, toothpaste and the hair goo *borrowed* from Mr. Nowell off the shelf in the bathroom. She adds deodorant, reminding him to use it after showering and gives him two photos to show his mother. In one picture he rides Yago, the Nowells' palomino. The other shows him with Walter and Anne outside their school. Walter and Anne are twins and also Dakota Indians. "Is there anything else you need?" she asks.

"My eagle jacket." His knees jiggle. He's dared to ask.

"Oh," she gasps, frowns, and blinks. She tucks a lock of hair behind her ear.

"It's not my jacket, belongs to my brother, GW." *You stole it. Remember?*

"I don't know—" She taps her thumbnail against her front teeth making a clicking sound.

"What do you mean?"

"I don't know. This might not be the right time."

"Right time?" *You're crazy,* he moogles a shout. His shoulders tense and a lump forms in his throat. He swallows hard and feels the lump slide into to his chest.

"I don't know," she hesitates and touches her cheek. "There'll be lots going on with the move and all. The jacket might get lost." She snaps the knapsack shut. "I think not."

"Shit! Why?" He plants his heels ready to argue. His anger triggers a Jenny thought. *She'd ask, what's going on?* Jenny has this Samurai Code she calls *'Listening to Ants'*. Look and listen to what's going on. Ask yourself, what you want to happen and how can you make it so.

Mrs. Nowell's the ant. She's afraid I'll run, as if I need the jacket to run. If I did run, they'd kiss off the thousand Hamm pays them a month to keep me.

He crosses his arms and glares until she leaves the room, then he picks up the knapsack and throws it on the bed. *Hurrah Jenny for your Samurai code!*

SAMURAI CODE

"You lied to me," Danny folds into the front seat of Jenny's red Escort. "You promised I could go home for the summer and now you changed everythin'. What am I gonna do?" He drops his knapsack on the floor, plants his silver-toed cowboy boots against the floor board, locks his knees and grunts like Mr. Nowell when he doesn't agree. Danny pushes the seat back. "I did everythin' you asked—school, homework, didn't run and even gave up smokin'."

"Sorry Danny, you did good. But I didn't change anything. It's your mom's life that's changing." Jenny pats his knee. "She wants a new life for the two of you. She needs to go back to school and that's the way it is."

Although he's been in love with Jenny since sentenced to Hamm three years ago, he pushes her hand away. She has the best T & A, lifts weights and can outrun any of the other probation officers at the school. She's been there for him when he was really scared, taught him what she calls the Samurai way—a code of ethics to help him through the tough times. He had plans for the summer to get his dad back and be a family again.

Jenny revs the Escort's motor and moves onto County Road 24. Danny scrunches down in the seat, crosses his arms and rounds his shoulders. The ride from the Nowells to his mom's place takes three hours, up Highway 61 along the Mississippi

River through Reads Landing to Lake City. Jenny smiles at him and pats his knee again.

"Tell me what's new."

He wants to stay mad but can't. He relaxes and tells how Walter and Anne took him morel mushrooming along the river when the lilacs bloomed.

"Walter used a stick to chase the rattlesnakes away and I earned three-hundred dollars—bought Mr. Nowell's silver-toed boots." He looks down at his feet and taps his toes. "Have you ever eaten mushrooms?"

She nods 'yes'.

"Ugh!" He tells Jenny about learning to ride Yago, and how he adopted an owl who lost its ma before it learned to hoot. "The owl's like me, a foster kid. Yesterday the crows attacked him 'cause he didn't get home before mornin'. Sort'a like bein' truant and havin' the principal report ya." He snickers and watches her smile at his joke.

"Mr. Nowell says owls eat baby crows. So the crows attacked and tried to make the owl leave his nest. Mr. Nowell calls it 'breaking cover' and then—" Danny claps his hands together. "Murder."

"Oh, my," Jenny makes a sad face. "And if the owl stays and doesn't break cover, will it be okay?"

Danny nods.

"When will it learn to hoot?"

"When it's time to procreate." He watches for Jenny's reaction. "Mr. Nowell says procreate, he never says the other word, though he probably can—he was a marine."

Jenny looks at Danny and smiles. Her blue eyes melt his heart. He sits quietly, squirming further into the seat as a warm buzz moves through his body.

As Jenny approaches Lake City, he sits up and opens his window. He sniffs the breeze coming from across Lake Pepin. West of the city, the road twists up through a canyon of orange-colored limestone, then levels out between newly plowed fields that come July, will be rows and rows of green corn stalks.

"When I get back, I'm going to sell my boots to Mr. Nowell. He promised to pay me three-hundred dollars if I kept them in good shape."

"Have you?"

"Ya bet."

"So, what are you going to do with all that money?"

"I don't know." He's moogled about buying a TV commercial. He likes commercials. His commercial would feature a kid wearing a Twins T-shirt, blue jeans and silver-toed cowboy boots. The kid would sit on a stool, play a guitar and recite a haiku:

Looking for my dad
Help me find him please and then
Send him home to me

Home Visit

JENNY TURNS OFF the ignition, and the Escort's engine chugs to a stop. Danny's mom waves from the front porch, where she is smoking and rocking in a wooden chair that once belonged to his grandmother before she died. A broken sidewalk leads from the street to the house. Grass grows between the cracks. The narrow, gray-shingled house needs painting. Purple violets and yellow dandelions dot the yard.

No trouble gettin' smokes here, Danny moogles. He flexes his eyebrows like Groucho on TV, who has a secret word that makes a bird fall out of the sky. His mom bounds down the steps and runs towards the car, her gray sweater flying open.

"Been waitin'," she says and tugs the car door open. Danny untangles his feet from the knapsack and unwinds out of the car. He feels guilty, as if it's his fault that they've arrived late. His mother wraps her arms around him and squeezes tight. His belly gulps for air, he pushes her away and she staggers backward.

"Why can't I stay?" He steadies her, but at the same time quivers with a sudden urge to shake her. "I did everythin' so I could stay home this summer. You ain't fair!"

"Oh Danny, I'm goin' ta school. I'm makin' us a new life." She jerks her arm out of his grip. Her face glows, her cheeks are smooth and pink. She smells different, both smoky and sweet. She shakes her head so her brown curls bounce. She reaches to touch him, but he turns away. A surge of anger pulses within him and he pulls his arm back to hit her, but stops as he feels the heat of Jenny's stare.

"You're a liar!" He grumbles, crosses his arms and tucks his hands under his arm pits. He stands stiff-legged to keep from trembling. *A GD liar.* He doesn't dare say the words with Jenny so close.

"Danny, stop!" Jenny steps beside him and taps his shoulder. She looks at him and her eyes command, "*listen.*"

"I wanted to stay the summer, not just this weekend," he blubbers. "You promised. I did everythin' you asked—" Tears slide down his cheeks. His legs say "*run.*"

"I know you did." Jenny reaches across his back in a gentle hug and cups his shoulder in a firm grip. She guides him toward the porch matching her step to his. His mother follows, sits back in the rocking chair and tosses her cigarette over the porch railing. Danny and Jenny sit side by side on a packing box. He likes her smell, soap from Hamm. She makes him feel safe.

"Danny," his mother begins, "the good news is I'm goin' ta school. The bad news is Joe's has closed. I lost my job."

"So?" He glares at her. "I can still hang around. I got friends. I can sleep…watch TV…." *Smoke without naggin.* He looks over the railing and watches the cigarette's smoke circling up through the grass. *If Jenny were gone, I'd grab the stick and run.*

"I know," his mom says, "but without a job, I can't stay here. I can't pay the rent. I'm movin' closer to school. I'm goin' ta be like you, learnin' stuff." She stifles a cough. "I'm learnin' computers. It's hard, but someday, I'll earn real money and we can be together." She primps her curly hair.

She's bad, Danny moogles, *she made my dad run away.*

Jenny stands and asks, "Everything going to be okay here?" Danny and his mother nod. "Then, I'll say goodbye. I'll be at the apartment tomorrow at four." She motions Danny to walk her to the Escort. "Do what you're asked," she says. She stares at him hard. "Be Samurai. No calls from your mom or the cops."

IN AND OUT

"THE HOUSE FEELS small." Danny stomps into the living room, circles around and looks at the stacks of boxes that fill the room. The afternoon sun filters through his grandmother's lace curtains that cool the room. He shivers. His grandmother rented the house long before his mom and dad moved in, before his dad left.

"You've just grown," his mother teases. "You're at least a foot taller than at Christmas. You're going to be tall and handsome, just like your—" She doesn't say the word.

"Guess so," he agrees. "Mrs. Nowell bought me new clothes, blue jeans and T-shirts. Even my feet are growin'. Soon my boots won't fit." He sticks out his foot. She glances down.

He tells her about hunting mushrooms and searching for rattlesnakes. He recounts the events in a lively description, stalking the slithery creatures using whispers, shouts, and raising his arms above his head. She hugs her gray sweater close to her chest. He tells her about buying the boots, but not about GW's jacket.

"I'm going to sell the boots back to Mr. Nowell for three-hundred dollars. Then, I think I'll buy a horse or a hog." He bends forward, thrusts out his fists and roars, pretending he's riding a motorcycle. His mother frowns.

"Oh—" Her voice fades to a whisper. She coughs.

Danny pulls the cord dangling from the ceiling and turns on a light. The yellow glow warms the room. He falls into the oversized, brown-vinyl chair in front of the television, where he and his mom once snuggled together, ate buttery popcorn and watched old movies after closing up Joe's. Then they'd sleep late, and naturally, he'd miss school.

"I left your stuff. Didn't know what you wanted to keep." She points to the ceiling above.

He jumps up, moves through the kitchen and climbs a steep stairway. He hasn't been home for five months. Inside his old room, he closes the door, pulls up the roller shade on the window and looks out. The window panes are dusty. He draws smiley faces on them with his finger, and then, sits on his bed and bounces. His knees touch the four-drawer dresser. In the top drawer, he flicks at a dried cigarette butt under some underwear. When he lies down and stretches, his boots touch the wall. He rubs his nose into his pillow. The familiar smell stirs his thoughts, a murder of thoughts like a gang of crows summoning more crows. He squeezes his eyes shut and thinks about Jenny and her Samurai code: what do you want to happen and how can you make it so.

Home and mom's movin'
But here is where he'd find me
Tell, what can I do?

Squirreled under the nest of bedcovers, he sniffs again the familiar smell and falls asleep, shutting out the world and feeling safe.

An hour later, a noise from downstairs awakens him. He rolls to his side and turns on a lamp clamped to the bedpost. He sits up, opens each dresser drawer and tosses the contents beside him: old T-shirts, outgrown shorts, and metallic cars he played with when he was six. There's a hacky sack *borrowed* from Target. He tosses the leather into the air. His mom was clueless, too dumb to know the hacky sack hid in her pocket. The guard threatened to arrest her and told her to *'never come back.'*

"Crap, all crap." He sweeps the stuff onto the floor and kicks it under the bed.

Downstairs, Danny finds his mother sitting at the kitchen table sipping coffee and smoking.

"Are you hungry?" she asks. "Want some supper?" She points to a box of cereal on the counter.

Danny sits and shakes his head '*no*.' He looks around. The bare green walls reveal strange bright spots where his grandmother's hot pads hung. He sees his mother's cigarettes and matches.

"Tell me about the Nowells." His mother moves her chair closer. She wears small gold earrings and pink lipstick.

"They're people, I guess. They live on the Mississippi River across from Wisconsin. Poison ivy grows everywhere. Big, blackwater bugs crawl up the walls and on every path I gotta watch for rattlesnakes." He watches her inhale and blow out a smoke ring. "There ain't no cars, and no street lights. *No sidewalks with cracks to break your mother's back.*

"Do you like them?"

He shrugs and makes a quirky face. "They don't watch TV much, just the news and college basketball, or the weather channel if there's gonna be a storm." *Never Hulk Hogan or The Claw.*

"Are they nice?"

"They're okay, they get a thousand bucks a month to keep me." He hesitates to say that their house is better than hers, or that Mrs. Nowell makes waffles, pizzas and brownies. He eyes his mother's cigarettes and matches. "But here I can do what I want when I want."

"Oh," she sighs, then, coughs. He knows she wants to know more, but he's antsy. He wants to go, not run away, just get out and look around. *Maybe everythin's not changin'.* He pushes back his chair.

"I'm out of here." He grabs her cigarettes and matches and walks out. He slams the kitchen door hard.

Meeting Places

DANNY WALKS BEHIND the house to a small barn, kicking through the tall grass that needs mowing. He squeezes the rusty latch on what was once a red door. Nothing happens. He steps back and lunges forward with a Samurai charge. The door groans and falls to one side. His old Hiawatha three-speed rests against the back wall. He wheels it into the fading daylight, brushes a settling of dust off the tired seat and sneezes. The tires are flat. He pushes the bike toward Speedy's.

"Need air," he calls through Speedy's open front door. The neighborhood's one-stop shop looks the same as before going to Hamm. A refrigerator, stacked with pizzas, cheeses, cold meats and sodas, sits beside a white-metal bread rack. He smells a box of apples on the counter. He remembers watching the owner tile the floor.

A kid about his age stands behind the counter. Danny looks at him hard, moogling, *is he from the old gang—or? Naw! Hair's too short.*

"Help yourself." The kid points to the air hose set back from a gas pump.

"Thanks." Danny eyes an apple. *That's what I'll do.* He pumps the tires and wheels the bike into the garage. "Got any oil?" he yells.

The kid comes to the garage door and points to an oilcan.

Tires hang on the wall along with pictures of girls in shorts and tight blouses, all bending over. Danny feels the kid watching. *Thinks I stole it.*

"Ain't been rid for years—parked in my grandma's shed."

"Oh," the kid says. He watches Danny oil the bike's chain, the bearings and pedals. When Danny finishes, he steps back and slaps the dirt off his hands. The kid points to a roll of paper towels.

"How long you been workin' here?" Danny cleans his hands and rubs his nose with his fist.

"Two months," the kid answers. "After three, I get a uniform shirt."

"Ya ever been robbed?" Danny tosses the paper towel in a trash bin.

"No, but I got a gun."

"A real gun?"

"With bullets."

"Ever shot a gun?"

The kid shakes his head.

"Neither have I. Can I see it?"

"Well," the kid pauses. "It ain't really my gun, belongs to the owner. He works nights." The kid motions Danny behind the counter and rings up a 'no sale'. He opens the cash drawer and shows Danny the gun. Danny swallows. He wants to touch it. He can hear the Hamm guys holler, *Whooee! Hot!* His knees jiggle.

"Wanna hold it?" the kid asks.

"Well," Danny pauses. He wants to. He looks up like he's counting ceiling tiles and hears Jenny's voice float down. *'Look where you are. What's going on? What do you want to happen?'*

Suddenly the kid moves behind him blocking the counter's opening. Danny feels trapped. A rush of panic burns his gut and he slams the cash drawer shut. *The kid's a fool or too damn smart. Gotta get out of here—fast!* He elbows the kid out of his way, grabs his bike, and pedals toward Joe's Bar. His heart beats triple time. *Jenny'd be mad as hell if I touched it, but the guys at Hamm would call me chicken.* He can hear them, '*Chicken! Chicken! Cluck! Cluck! Cluck!*'

He bikes past Joe's. Last summer the windows flashed with neon beer signs. Now the windows are black. Since second grade, he's helped his mom at Joe's: washed glasses, wiped ashtrays, and swept the floor. He also smoked cigarette butts left in ashtrays, drank warm beer left in brown bottles, and when no one was looking, pocketed his mom's tips.

He pedals past the post office, the drug store, a new insurance building and into the park. He balances the bike between his legs. He inhales then exhales, counts to ten and looks around. The trees seem to stand closer together than what he remembers. He smells roses. Nearby, a bronze statue of an ancient war hero rides a horse and commands his concrete base. Sometimes his gang climbed behind the man, one guy, two or three. The newest guy got on last, waited to be pushed off and called the 'horse's ass.' Sometimes the gang crawled under the horse's belly and smoked. If someone had money, they bought Marlboros or Old Golds. If not, they crumbled up leaves and rolled them in newspaper. Sometimes the gang sipped *magic hooch.* Danny collected the magic at Joe's from near-empty bottles, all colors, smells and tastes. When the hooch bottle was full, he brought it to the park. There, the gang sipped the magic to find true insight and planned bank robberies smarter than Jesse James, so they wouldn't get caught.

The park's yellow lanterns flick on. Danny finds a bench, sits down and lights up a cigarette, tossing the spent match on the sidewalk. Since living on the river, he now hears night sounds. Crickets chirp. A katydid rubs its legs. At the Nowells', he'd also hear leopard frogs zinging like fingernails zipping a pocket comb.

He rolls the smoke stick between his fingers and then draws it close to his lips. He inhales, chokes, gasps and tears run down his cheeks.

"Damn her." He reaches under his shirt, pulls off the nicotine patch Mrs. Nowell insists he wear, and throws it beneath the bench. He holds the cigarette out like a candle and thinks about the gun and the kid at Speedy's. He thinks about Jenny and her Samurai code. He thinks about being home tonight and not being able to stay.

Home for the night so
GW's comin', mom's movin'
Everything's changin'

Home for the night then
Get me a gun and leave fast
River here I comes

OLD WAYS

A CAR ROUNDS the corner, slows and stops. Danny's instinct screams 'cops'. The driver gets out and slams the door. Danny watches the bulky shadow lumber toward him. He pinches off the burning end of the smoke stick and grinds it out on the sidewalk with the heel of his boot. Then with one hand hanging loose beside him, he strips the tobacco to the ground and stuffs the paper and the filter into his pocket, next to the twenty-dollar bill from Mrs. Nowell. He slouches down on the bench, stretching his legs out in front of him.

Sittin' here peaceful
Here comes the man figurin'
Once bad, always bad

"Well, if it isn't Danny Malloy," the cop says. "Figured you'd be home, with your mom movin' and everythin'. How've ya been?"

"Okay," Danny answers. He sits up and kicks the nicotine patch with his boot. *No need to give him a reason to get me.*

"Still at Hamm?"

"Sort'a."

"Keepin' your nose clean?"

"Yup."

"That's good." The cop sits beside him and wiggles his backside over more than half the bench. He smells of salami. "So, what's new?"

"Not much. My mom's movin', like you said."

"Too bad about Joe's."

"Ya, I was hopin' ta work there this summer."

"Ah." The cop's voice goes up. "So whatcha doin' for money?"

"Plan to sell my boots." Danny lifts his leg and twists his foot so the park lanterns reflect their yellow lights on the silver-toes.

"Pretty fancy," the cop agrees.

"Ya, they're worth three-hundred dollars."

"Where'd you get them?"

"From my foster dad."

"Did you steal them? Or like you always said, ya borrowed them?"

"No, I bought them with money I earned. But he's goin' to buy them back. They're gettin' too small."

"You tellin' me you worked?" The cop rocks the bench, pushing his hands down on his thighs, stretching his neck and flexing his shoulders.

"Well, I picked mushrooms. I call it work. Gotta be careful of the rattlesnakes."

"Don't we all?" Danny feels the man grin into the dark.

Suddenly the night is silent, as if all the creatures in the park hear the message, 'Bad is bad'. The cop stands and offers his hand. "Good luck, Danny boy. Sorry your mom's movin'. She's a nice lady."

Danny watches the cop waddle back to his car. *Even he's changin', gettin' old and senile, maybe blind. Called my mom a lady.* Danny snorts. *Didn't call her a lady, when he put me in Hamm.* He waits until the patrol car leaves, then lights up another cigarette, inhales and spits out the bad taste in his mouth. He rolls the smoke stick between his fingers and watches the smoke rise.

Danny Malloy, Samurai Summer

Get a gun and cash
Go Samurai, zip out fast
Home ain't here no more

A Safe Place

MORNING SUNLIGHT HIGHLIGHTS the smiley faces on the dirty window panes. Danny opens his eyes and kicks the sheet to the end of the bed. He stretches long and wide. His toes touch the wall at the end of the bed and his fingertips touch the wall and the dresser. Once, this was his safe place. Then, something happened.

He remembers hiding his head under his pillow, months of trying not to hear the loud voices in the kitchen below: GW and his dad, GW and his mom, his dad and his mom. And then, one day, everything was quiet and his dad left. The memory stings his eyes. He moans and rocks his body from side to side. *Why did I work so hard to come home?*

After he left the park last night, he biked back to Speedy's. The kid was gone and the owner was cleaning up. The guy called him by name.

"Well, if it ain't Danny Malloy," he said. He was wiping the counter with a spray and cloth. "They let you out for a visit?"

"Guess, you can say that." Danny watched as the old man polished the cash drawer. When the fingerprints were gone, he used Mrs. Nowell's twenty to buy pizza and soda. Then he went home, helped his mom bake the pizza and they watched an old movie about a dumb crook who got caught. He'd borrowed an apple from Speedy's counter. It sat next to his boots on the dresser.

The window shade moves, pushed by a gentle breeze. Voices float up the stairs. He vaguely recalls hearing a hog. GW. He swings out of bed, pulls on his boots and hurries down the steps.

"Greetings, Li'l Bro, put it there." He squeezes Danny's hand. GW wears a big silver ring and black boots with silver buckles. GW's leather vest frames a gold rope that holds a medallion tucked in a mass of curls on his bare chest. He's ten years older than Danny, an alumnus of Hamm. He fixes hogs. GW grabs Danny in a hug that hurts and spins him around. "Good grief Li'l Bro, you've gotten tall."

A blonde sits at the kitchen table. She wears a yellow blouse that flows off her shoulders and swoops across her bosoms. Her long fingernails shine bright red.

Danny pours a cup of coffee, dumps in some milk and two spoonfuls of sugar. His mother pushes a box of donuts toward him. He chooses a chocolate iced with fudge frosting and sprinkled with crushed nuts.

"I'm Bobbie with an *ie*," the woman says, "and this is my breakfast." She holds up a hard-boiled egg. "Can't take the sugar." She salts the egg, bites, and licks her fingers. She stands and wipes her fingers on her jean legs. "Nice to meet you," she says and shakes Danny's hand.

Danny notes her motorcycle boots with silver buckles. He holds her hand, bowing and flashing his charming smile. "Nice to meet you, too." He stares at her soft, round breasts.

Bobbie blushes and peeks coyly over her shoulder at GW.

"So, the kid's got good taste." GW shrugs his shoulder and grins.

Soon all four sit at the table, drinking coffee and smoking. GW and Danny recount their trip to Deadwood the last summer. GW promises Danny a summer trip to Sturgis this year with Bobbie. Then, GW looks at his watch.

"Time to work," he says.

A van appears in front of the house. Danny and Bobbie move boxes. While they lift and carry, she talks about real things—riding motorcycles and trips to the Dakotas. She asks what he wants to do when he graduates from high school. *She'll be fun on our trip to Sturgis. I need to buy motorcycle boots.*

After moving boxes, Danny helps GW pile all the house trash into black garbage bags. Upstairs, they sit and rest on Danny's bare mattress.

"How will he find us?" Danny asks.

"Who?" GW looks puzzled.

"You know who!" Danny's cheeks flush and he chokes on the word. "Dad."

GW scratches his cheek. "Danny. Oh, Danny," he moans softly. "He can find us anytime if he wants. But he ran away, ran away from mom, from me, from you. He ran away from himself."

"Ain't you ever heard from him?"

GW shakes his head.

"What'd we do wrong?"

"Nothin'. Like I said, he just ran away."

"But, I gotta strange feelin', leavin' here without him knowin'."

"Ya, but, its okay. If he'd come back, folks 'round here know where to find us."

"Don't you ever miss him?"

"Naw, didn't know him e'nuf ta' miss him." GW sighs and his shoulders slump. "Anyway, Li'l Bro, you got me, we're family." GW gives Danny a reassuring pat on the back. "But we gotta get a move on."

Together they pick up the mattress, shove it through the doorway, and laugh as they wrestle it down the steep stairway on their bellies. By afternoon, his mom's new apartment is stacked with all the boxes. She lives close to her school and a shopping center. Danny helps her unpack kitchen utensils and tacks up some of his grandma's crocheted hot pads. GW and Bobbie arrange the brown rocker and the television in the living room and set up her bed in a small bedroom. When the move is finished, they sit down at the kitchen table, talking, laughing, drinking coffee, smoking and eating hoagies bought at a nearby deli.

At six o'clock, two hours late, Jenny knocks on the apartment door. Danny gives his mom a wave good-bye then turns to Bobbie. He wraps his arm around her waist and walks his fingers into her back pocket. She blushes and rubs her hip bone against him.

"Nice ta have met you," she whispers. Her moist lips tickle his ear and a rush zips through his body making him warm.

Danny sees Jenny raise her eyebrows.

EVERYTHING'S CHANGIN'

DANNY SLIPS INTO the Escort beside Jenny, kicking aside the knapsack he'd left on the floor. She starts the engine and gives him a smile. "You okay?" He nods and watches her steer the car onto the highway, shifting through the gears and humming to herself. He falls asleep and dreams about being an owl learning to hoot.

On Monday morning, Danny's up with the sun doing barn chores and setting mouse traps. His owl didn't break cover. He swings on the lower part of the split barn door and looks up into a dome of blue crossed with white contrails. He slides the disappointment of not going home for the summer into a part of his heart reserved for hurts. Often his hurts get twisted with thoughts of running.

Today, I'll stay. I'll be Samurai. Today is a good day to ask for a bike and motorcycle boots with thick soles and silver buckles. What happened with mom, happened. I'll think about what I want and how to make it so, like goin' to Sturgis or findin' another way to get my dad back home.

After a pizza and salad lunch, the Nowells take Danny to the bicycle shop. He shops for a bike, and eyes a used Trek, a mountain bike with 27 speeds and disc brakes. Dark red.

"It's speed," the salesman says. "Can do thirty-five miles an hour, more going down hill. Front and rear brakes and a flip flop hub that gives you the option to go freewheeling or hard core gearing. Will keep you a spinning and grinning." The salesman grins.

It ain't a motorcycle, Danny moogles, *but I bet I could bike all the way to Sturgis.*

Mrs. Nowell rolls her eyes and writes a check.

"Can I have boots too, with silver buckles and real thick soles?" Danny asks.

Mr. Nowell smiles and says he'll think about it.

Samurai Name

On Tuesday morning after breakfast and chores, Danny dusts the Trek with a pink towel borrowed from the linen closet. He checks the chain, rocks the bike back and forth, mounts the seat and pedals around and around the backyard doing circles and singing, "My name is Danny, Danny Malloy. See me touch the sky." He stretches his arms into the crystal air. Tuesday's sun promises to shine all day.

"I'm Samurai," he shouts. According to Jenny, the Samurai were special because they had names, real names, not like other people who were called by what they did or who owned them.

"My name is Danny Malloy." His blue cotton shirt billows behind him. He holds out his arms and steers the bike with his knees, a cool rush of air tickles his underarms.

He'd borrowed deodorant this morning from Mr. Nowell's shelf in the bathroom and combed his hair for ten minutes, parting it every which way to look older. Soon he'd have hair on his chest and chin. He'd need to shave, and that meant buying a razor, a Gillette, a double-blade like Mr. Nowell's.

Danny can hardly wait to show Walter the bike. He wants to go *spinning and grinning*. He also wants to escape Mrs. Nowell, who suggested at breakfast that her flowers need weeding.

He leaves the backyard and pedals past the stable with its lush green pasture bordered by tall pine trees. Yago looks up from munching with an eye that gives Danny a pinch of conscience for choosing the bike. Danny makes a silent pledge to feed the horse an extra scoop of oats.

County Road 24, called CR 24 by the Nowells, curves west to Highway 30, away from the Mississippi River and toward the high bluffs carved by the river in an ancient age. Black shadows creep down the steep sides, sliding over pines, oaks, sumac and outcroppings of limestone as the sun climbs high in the sky. Miles behind him the green dragon rests atop a Wisconsin bluff. His Samurai dragon.

CR 24 dips where it crosses a culvert. In the spring, or when the river runs high, the culvert links the backwater to a meadow seeded by the DNR, the Department of Natural Resources. *"Government people,"* Mr. Nowell calls them.

The backwater is part of the old Zumbro River that once flowed into the Mississippi three miles upstream through the town of Wabasha, but has changed course several times in the last hundred years. Now it flows into the Mississippi near the village of Kellogg.

Turtles leave the old Zumbro backwater and cross the road by the culvert to lay their eggs in the DNR's grass. If the turtles were smart, they'd crawl through the culvert, but they're not. Danny scans the road ahead for dead turtles and vultures eating a road-kill breakfast. The mothers have crossed the road safely. At this time of year, turtles seem to be everywhere.

CR 24 ends at Highway 30. Danny turns and looks ahead for more turtles. *Mother turtles are dumb to cross the road,* Danny moogles. *Fathers are smarter. They stay home.*

On Highway 30 he passes his high school, then, he turns toward the river on a gravel road that edges what once was the county's poor farm. Walter says the cemetery behind the farm is now planted in corn but the Indian mounds nearby have been left untouched. Walter doesn't know who is buried in the Indian mounds because the Dakota who lived on the river a hundred years ago didn't bury their dead. They put them on platforms hung in the trees. Walter knows all about Indians; he's a Sioux, his mother comes from the Lakota family and his dad is Dakota.

Danny pedals into the Goulette clearing no-handed, raises a war-hoop, loud and powerful, imitating Walter when he chants and beats his drum. "Whoo Hee! Whoo Hee! Haiya Haiya Whoo Hee. I'm Danny Malloy, Samurai," he yells.

WHATCHA DOIN'?

THE GOULETTE LODGE, a long room made of bent saplings covered with white canvas, looks deserted. Waves on the nearby Mississippi River reflect dancing mirrors of sunlight and lap against the shore with a steady rhythm. A wren sings a cheerful song and a cardinal wolf whistles. A couple of squirrels chatter to each other from the tall oaks.

Charlie, a boxer-retriever mix, guardian of the camp, climbs down his ladder, greets Danny with a bark and licks his fingers. The dog won a prize at the county fair for climbing ladders. Anne steps through the lodge's doorway.

"Walter's gone fishing with my dad," she says. She's tall and thin like her twin, but unlike her brother she wears her dark hair short. Walter sports a pony tail. Anne wears two earrings, he wears one. Walter boasts about his French-Indian heritage, his great, great grandfather, a French trapper, married the daughter of a Dakota chief. Anne is quiet and writes poems about being an American. She won first prize for a Memorial Day poem, got twenty-five dollars and a chance to read it in front of everybody. Today, she wears blue jean shorts, a red shirt and white Nikes.

"Whatcha doin'?" he asks, wheeling the Trek close beside her.

"Turtles." She smiles. "Nice." She strokes the bike's handlebars.

"Brand new, anyway to me. Sold my boots to Mr. Nowell."

"Oh." She raises her eyebrows.

"So, whatcha doin'?" he asks again.

"Turtles. The Blandings are crossing the road at Weaver.

"Turtles?" he groans.

"They need help," Anne says. "Want to come with me—on a turtle mission?"

"Nope," he shakes his head, "don't think so." Walter scolds at Danny when they canoe and Danny throws stones at the lazy shells sunning on logs. Walter calls them *"old mothers"*, says Danny should give them respect. "Nope, turtles ain't my thing."

A few nights ago, he'd watched a mean looking snapper, big as a black dishpan, crawl up the river bank. The old mother had circled the yard, chose her spot and ripped up the grass, throwing dirt five feet out with dagger-like claws. Then she eased back into the hole and dropped a pile of white eggs. He'd watched, embarrassed. After the snapper left, another turtle, saucer-sized, flat, shiny-green, with an orange-red belly, plodded onto the circle. That mother nestled her rear into the soft dirt and spewed out eggs with her eyes shut. Danny watched the egg-laying process until dark. He thought it was disgusting.

"We're getting a turtle nursery," Mrs. Nowell said. "We have a snapper and paint. Now we need a Blanding."

"What's a Blanding?" Danny asked.

"A rare turtle that looks like an army helmet," she said. "They have a high-domed shell, olive in color. Once, they stopped a power plant from being built at McCarthy Lake.

"The turtles?"

"No, not the turtles, silly," she teased, "but the people who cared." She frowned at him with a good-humored scowl. "The Blandings live at McCarthy Lake but lay their eggs in the Weaver Dunes, south of Kellogg. They were and still are endangered, if you think about cars."

She explained how the Blandings cross the highway from the lake to the dunes, gravid turtles she called them, females with eggs. After laying their eggs, the mothers go back to the lake. Then in the fall, the

*babies migrate from the dunes to McCarthy, crossing the highway—
that is if the skunks and possums haven't dug up the eggs.*
Mrs. Nowell jumped at her words, "Skunks and possums!" She
waved for him to follow and in the garage she found two bushel
baskets. *"We'll keep the eggs covered until the rains wash away the
smell,"* she said.

Now, Danny moogles, *Anne wants me to rescue old mother
turtles.* He looks at Anne, leans on his bike and strokes the chrome
handle bars. He swats at a mosquito buzzing his ear. *But with
Walter gone fishing, what else can I do?* He slaps at the bug. *Go
back to Nowells and weed.*

"Oh, come on," Anne coaxes, "you need to ride your bike.
You need to get your legs in shape. Walter can do more than
twenty-five miles."

TURTLE MISSION

ANNE LEADS THE way. She pedals fast but not as fast as the cars on Highway 61 that zip by. Danny reins in the temptation to pass her and watches her long legs keep a steady rhythm. The railroad track runs along the east side of the four-lane highway. A morning Amtrak buzzes past sounding an eerie warning for crossings down the line.

In Kellogg they pass the post office, the bank, and then turn south past the fire station and Curly's Bait Shop, where Mr. Nowell buys willowcats for catching northerns. Curly is as bald as a bowling ball and has a hundred stories to tell. They turn on CR 84 and pass houses with long driveways, each with a wood pile ready for the next winter.

Eight miles beyond Kellogg, Anne stops beside the Weaver Dunes sign and lifts two water bottles from her bike's basket. Danny balances his bike between his legs, swipes his shirt sleeve across his forehead and gasps for breath. His knees burn, but he's not sure if it's from pedaling or sunburn. His calves feel as if he's biked a hundred miles. He counts to ten then takes the bottle of water, tipping it up for a long swig. The coolness slides down his throat. He empties the rest of the water on his chest and waits for Anne to scold his wastefulness. Instead, she does the same.

She blushes and sighs. The water deepens the red of her shirt inching across her chest like a pool of blood. The cloth clings to the mounds of her breasts. Her nipples shove against the shirt like hard, sharp buttons. *Geeze,* he moogles, *she's becoming a woman.* He wants to pluck them, the thought makes him blush.

For the next hour, they wheel their bikes between two *'rare turtle'* signs, one by the dunes and the other by Schmoker's Bridge, a stone bridge that crosses Snake Creek a mile south. They find one Blanding leaving the dunes. Anne picks her up and shows Danny the turtle's yellow chin and throat. He watches the old mother retreat into her shell, what Mrs. Nowell called a carapace.

Anne puts the Blanding down on the lake side of the road. No more turtles cross. No cars whiz by. The sun climbs high in the sky.

They park their bikes by the stone bridge. The narrow creek, headed for the Mississippi from McCarthy Lake, rushes through a stand of oaks and scrub. Danny and Anne search out a patch of grass and sit down. He stretches his legs and lies back, resting his head on his crossed arms. He squeezes his eyes shut and wishes he'd worn a cap. A deer fly nips his elbow. Anne sits beside him. She plops a new bottle of water on his stomach.

Once she gave me smoke sticks. Walter said she'd had a vision, and in her vision she'd met a brother who needed smokes. Walter figured the brother was me.

But Anne's supply of smoke sticks stopped when her aunt quit smoking. Danny missed smoking, but he didn't miss Mrs. Nowell's hassle and he hated her damn nicotine patches.

A mosquito buzzes Danny's ear. He swats the air. Everything seems quiet, spooky quiet. He's glad when Anne starts talking like a travel log. She tells how the Blandings stopped the building of a power plant, the same story Mrs. Nowell told. After she talks about Blandings, she continues to tell about the Weaver Dunes. "They're old, a special place, with rare birds, butterflies, flowers and plants. The grasses that grow there are like the grasses pioneers traveled through on their way west to settle Minnesota. The dunes are like my people found them."

Danny sits up. "You're amazing. How do you know all that stuff?"

"I'm Dakota, remember. We're one with nature."

Her shirt has dried. Her nipple buttons have disappeared. *But, she'll grow boobs,* he moogles, *and I'll grow a beard.* The thoughts make his body warm. He wants to touch her, so he pokes her belly. She hits him off and soon they tussle, rolling in the grass. He pins her down, and holds her arms stretched out. He likes the sweet smell of her breath and the way she twists beneath him. He wants to kiss her but she pushes hard, breaks away and stands up.

"I'm glad you came with me," she says, "but it was just for turtles." He watches her wiggle as she mounts her bike.

Old Momma

Anne and Danny leave the Weaver Dunes and their Blanding turtle mission. They bike through Kellogg and head north over the bridge on Highway 61 that spans the Zumbro River. On the road ahead, a black turtle moves like a robot-action figure, legs arched out, a dinosaur beak protruding from a bullet-shaped head.

Anne slows and stops on the gravel shoulder. Danny brakes in a puff of dust.

"Snapper," Anne says, "probably wants to cross the highway. She'll lay her eggs up there." Danny follows Anne's finger as she points. The highway is cut into the river bluff. South-bound traffic moves at a higher elevation than the north-bound traffic. A clump of birch, oak and scrub divides the lanes.

"How do we get her off the road?" Danny asks.

"If we drag her to the trees, she won't stay," Anne says. "We need to move her all the way across the four lanes." Anne puts her hands on her hips and frowns.

"How do we drag her?" Danny approaches the turtle. She's as big as the Snapper on the river bank he watched laying eggs. She rears and snarls, slashing the air with her long razor claws. He jumps. "She's an angry momma," he says. The turtle hisses and lashes toward him. "She could bite my finger off."

"I wish we had a shovel," Anne says. "We could scoop her up and carry her across."

"But we don't."

"Maybe we could push her," Anne says.

"I'll find a branch." Danny climbs the steep embankment between the lanes, kicking grasses aside with each step, wary of rattlesnakes. He stumbles through a ring of low growing oak, honeysuckle and buckthorn and notes the shiny leaves of poison ivy. The trees shade the ground and the air smells cool. He finds a downed branch with a sweep of leaves and slides down the embankment to Anne.

The old snapper still claws the air, fighting mad. Her eyes shine with black fire. Her shell is covered with a dried-on green slime.

Danny moves behind her. The snapper wheels to attack. Danny swishes the branch. The turtle lunges, avoids the branch, and reaches for Danny. He steps back. She snarls and spits, her claws just miss him. He retreats again. She snaps and snarls, this time attacking the branch with a vengeance. Their battle moves to the middle of the road. *This momma ain't gonna hide in no shell,* Danny moggles.

"Danny!" Anne screams, "Move!" Two semis barrel toward him, coming fast with their horns blaring. Anne grabs his shirt and they tumble into the ditch as the tug of the trucks sucks the air around them. The trucks leave the turtle smushed.

DEAD MOMMA

"The ole momma is dead!" Danny untangles himself from Anne's arms and legs. He crawls out of the ditch and walks to the circle of carapace, egg shells and blood, her long black nails driven deep into the soft tarvy. Behind him, Anne sobs.

"It's so sad. We were just trying to help."

That mean momma got what she had coming, he moogles. He frowns at Anne.

"What are we going to do?" Anne wipes away a tear from her cheek.

"Do?"

"Yes, do." She looks at him with a *'you're so dumb stare'*. "We can't just leave her here. She's an old mother, a really old mother." She grabs the turtle's tail and pulls her toward the oaks. "We'll bury her." Anne's sobs turn to hiccups, she wipes her cheeks with her shirt sleeves and sniffs.

"A turtle is just a turtle," Danny argues, but Anne's sobs stop him. He looks at her. He's never seen a woman cry, except his mom, when the cop came to their house to put him in jail for borrowin' stuff. "I guess we can bury her, but we need a shovel." He hates feeling guilty.

An hour later, Danny and Anne return to the grove with a spade borrowed from the Nowells' garage. There is no embankment off the south-bound highway into the trees. They park their bikes just inside the tree line and find a level spot. The spade unfolds into a neat package, two-feet long, marked with a dab of green paint. Danny points to the green spot. Mr. Nowell marks his tools because his neighbors borrow but never return them until he hunts them down.

Danny uses the spade to clear a circle of last year's dead leaves and digs a hole. Anne tugs the snapper to the hole and Danny covers the grave with sand.

Anne sniffs with an occasional hiccup. Danny's legs throb. *Biking is harder than riding Yago,* he moogles, *bet I've ridden more than twenty-five miles.*

"We need to pray." Anne talks so softly that Danny can barely hear her.

"Pray?" He pokes his tongue inside his cheek doing a half-smirk.

"Yeah! Pray." She glares at him silently saying, '*Stupid*'.

Danny scratches his ear. "Pray?" Then he remembers. *Walter prays, beats a drum and sings his prayers the Dakota way.*

"She was an old turtle," Anne says. "She lived a long time."

"Maybe with the dinosaurs," Danny adds to make her smile. "The old turtle sure fought like a Samurai."

Anne kneels by the grave. "Old mother have a safe journey. Live with the brave warriors in the sky beyond the stars."

Sky Star. Danny kneels and touches Anne's hand. "Let's call her Sky Star. She died like a Samurai and all Samurai have names."

Anne brushes away a wet tear on her cheek. She prays in almost a whisper,

> "Old turtle journey
> Far and fast brave Sky Star
> Samurai warrior"

Danny feels a glow inside him. He remembers the turtle's last brave battle, her flashing eyes and clawing nails, how she lunged at him and snarled. Anne's prayer is the turtle's Samurai's death song. They stand and bow their heads.

"We need to keep the coons away," Danny says, after a minute. He steps onto the turtle's sandy grave and dances. Anne claps and dances with him.

TWO DEAD MOMMAS

DANNY PICKS UP the spade and leans it against a nearby tree. He sees the woman, an old lady sitting on the ground, her legs spread out in front of her. She leans against an oak tree, her black tie shoes tossed beside her. She wears a red and blue flowered dress and holds a big purse in her lap. Danny pokes Anne and points.

Anne moves toward the woman explaining about the turtle. The woman doesn't move.

"She must be sleeping," Danny whispers.

"I think she's dead," Anne whispers back, stepping behind Danny.

"What? How do you know?"

"She's not breathing. Her eyes are wide open."

Danny looks. Black eyes stare back at him as if they are fish eyes. Anne grabs his hand.

"What are we going to do?" Anne whispers.

"Do?"

"Yes, do!" She doesn't add stupid. "We have to tell somebody."

"Like who?"

"Like the sheriff, you dummy."

"You're crazy! I ain't gonna tell no sheriff," Danny protests. He pushes Anne away. "I'm a JD."

"A JD?"

"Ya, a JD, a juvenile delinquent."

"What does that matter?" Anne argues.

"It matters a lot. You ain't ever been in jail." He feels the heat of his blood pulsate in his head. He remembers his panic when the cell door slammed shut.

"But we have to tell somebody," Anne argues. She stands tall and lifts her shoulders as she breathes deeply. Danny sees she's determined.

"You can tell anyone you want," he shouts. "I'm leav'n. I'm gettin' the hell out of here."

A Sheriff's Visit

Flashing blue, red and white lights sweep through the Nowells' windows and across the yellow kitchen walls. Danny chokes on a swig of root beer. His knees shake. He puts his hands on his thighs to keep his legs from jiggling and watches Mr. Nowell answer the knock on the door.

Sheriff VanOort walks in, shakes hands with Mr. Nowell and says friendly words to Mrs. Nowell. Danny can't stop the jiggling in his legs. His ears buzz. The sheriff sits down at the table across from Danny, looks at him without saying a word. The sheriff's body seems to fill the room. His fists are the size of boxing gloves. He moves onto the chair as if he's settling in for the night and shifts his holster belt to one side. The belt holds a large, steel automatic, bullets, keys and a radio.

"Well Danny, seems you had some excitement today," the sheriff says, after what seems to be forever. His eyes blaze like lasers in a space flick.

Danny swallows a lump in his throat, shuddering as the hurt slides down to his belly. Mr. Nowell stares. Mrs. Nowell gasps and covers her mouth.

"Danny didn't tell you?" VanOort looks at the couple and raises his eyebrows. "He and the Goulette girl found a dead woman out on the highway. The girl came into my office about four this afternoon, sobbing her heart out."

"Danny?" the Nowells ask in unison.

What can I say? He feels trapped. His body tenses, a band around his forehead squeezes so tight spots dance before his eyes. He breathes in, counts to ten and looks at the ceiling. He crosses his arms over his chest, leans back and slides his butt to the edge of the chair. He balances on his boot heels. *The last time a sheriff looked at me like this, I landed in jail. Anne squealed. Damn her!*

The panic burns inside him, the gut pain he's felt before when accused of borrowing things, skipping school and talking back. He wants to run, but run smart so he doesn't get caught. He needs to use the bathroom, but VanOort's dagger eyes nail him.

"Talk," Mr. Nowell commands, using his marine voice. A tense cloud hovers over the table.

"Tell me," VanOort says. "What did you see?" The sheriff leans forward, his holster shifts against his hip.

Danny begins, talking so softly he can barely hear himself. "We saw a dead woman…leaning against a tree…holding her purse. Shoes kicked off, black shoes." He tries not to sound weepy. He's cautious, he's anxious. He remembers Jenny's Samurai code. *Pay attention to where you are. Listen to the small stuff. Stay cool. Ask for what you want to happen.*

"What was the woman wearing," the sheriff demands.

Danny shrugs. "I don't remember." He hears the Hamm guys' counsel, *Never trust a lawman.*

"Tell me about the purse."

"I don't remember." *Don't tell'm nothin'.*

"What color was it?"

Danny shrugs.

"How big?"

"I just remember it on her lap."

"What about her hands? What do you remember about her hands?"

"Nothing, just hands."

VanOort leans back in his chair.

"I'm not lyin'." Danny looks at the Nowells, who now stand

behind the sheriff. "I don't remember. I was scared. I just wanted to get out of there." He moves to get up, but again, VanOort's eyes stop him.

"Of course, kid," the sheriff agrees. "I'd been scared too, but I need to ask you some questions." The sheriff looks over his shoulder at Mr. Nowell, then back at Danny.

"Did you see anyone close by?" the sheriff asks.

"No."

"See anyone walking on the road?"

Danny shakes his head.

"Hear anyone talking?"

Danny shrugs and shakes his head. *No.*

"Where did you go when you left the woman?"

"Here, home to the Nowells."

"You live with the Nowells?"

Danny looks at the Nowells and nods. Mrs. Nowell wipes tears from her cheeks.

"You a foster kid?"

"Yes."

"Been in trouble before?"

Danny nods.

"So you came straight home?"

"Ya."

Mr. Nowell puts his arm around his wife's waist.

"Did you talk to anyone, tell them about the lady?"

Danny shakes his head. *The smoking Danny could have checked for cigarettes.* "I guess I was scared."

"You guess?"

"I was scared."

"You okay?" Mrs. Nowell touches Danny's shoulder.

"I don't remember. I didn't hurt her. I'm not a murderer. We just killed Sky Star."

"Sky Star?" VanOort looks at Mr. Nowell.

"Sky Star?" Mr. Nowell frowns.

"Ya, the dead turtle. We named her Sky Star, Anne and me."

"I think you better tell me everything." The sheriff holds up his cup and looks at Mrs. Nowell. Mrs. Nowell puts the coffee pot on the table and sits down. Mr. Nowell pulls his chair next to Danny and fills the sheriff's cup.

"I didn't kill nobody," Danny says, "except the old turtle."

"Of course you didn't." Mrs. Nowell rolls her cup between her hands. "The sheriff just needs to ask questions. He's doing his job."

But he don't like me, Danny moogles. *He's got it in for foster kids.*

"So tell me again. What do you know?" The sheriff leans forward in his chair and sips his coffee.

Danny breathes deeply, holding his legs to keep them from jiggling. He begins and tells what he remembers.

TWILIGHT VISIT

"WE NEED TO take a little trip." VanOort stands and adjusts the holster belt around his hips.

"Are you taking me to jail?" Danny blurts. Tears sting his eyes.

"No, no. Just want you and me to visit where you found the woman."

"I'm coming, too," Mr. Nowell says. Mrs. Nowell brushes away a stream of tears on her cheeks. Mr. Nowell hugs her. "Honey, it's going to be okay."

The sheriff waits by the door and ushers Danny into the back seat of the patrol car. Danny sees that like so many rides before Hamm, *there ain't no handles on the inside.*

Mr. Nowell slides onto the front seat next to the sheriff, grunts and slams his door. The sheriff revs the motor and heads toward Highway 61. Danny shuts his eyes. His heart beats a hundred miles a minute. His bladder aches. He hears the men talk about a fishing contest. He's scared and he moogles:

Be Samurai man
Don't break your cover or else
VanOort will get ya

The sheriff crosses the railroad and pulls alongside the highway near where Danny and Anne buried the turtle. The car's lights zip between the oak trees like frenzied ghosts. A yellow tape reflects the car's headlights.

Mr. Nowell opens his door. Danny waits for the sheriff.

"Tell me again," the sheriff says as they walk, bending under the tape that warns, *No trespassing, Crime Scene*. He flicks on a flashlight, though it's still light. "What did you see?"

Danny points to the tree where the woman rested. He describes how her shoes laid on the ground, kicked off. The sheriff shines his light on the tree.

"What was the woman wearing?"

Danny shrugs. "Don't remember." *Can't trust a lawman,* he hears the Hamm guys warn.

"Tell me about the purse."

"Think it was black." Danny shrugs again. *Remember, don't tell him nothin'.*

"How big?" The sheriff demands.

Danny shrugs once more. *This man causes harm, better be careful.*

"She was holdin' it on her lap."

"What about her hands? What do you remember about her hands?" Danny hears anger in the sheriff's voice. The lawman jiggles the keys in his pocket.

"Nothin', just hands. I was scared, I wanted out of here." *What can I do? How can I make this guy believe me? I just don't remember, but I ain't gonna lie.*

"Of course, kid, I'd been scared too," the sheriff says. "Just need to ask you these questions."

Mr. Nowell walks toward the sheriff and they exchange glances.

"A few years ago we found another lady here," the sheriff says. "Dead. Never did find out who she was. This time, it's different. The woman's local." He turns and looks at Danny. "Did you see anyone here?" he asks.

Danny shrugs.

"Speak up boy," the sheriff sounds tired. "See anyone close by?"

"No sir," Danny answers.

"See anyone walking on the road?"

"No sir," Danny answers.

"Hear anyone talking?"

"No sir."

"Where did you go when you left here?

"Home, to the Nowells." He wants to scream. *Told you. You're just gettin' to me bein' a foster kid.*

"You live with the Nowells?"

"Yes sir." Danny nods. Mr. Nowell steps closer to Danny.

"You a foster kid?"

"Yes sir."

"Been in trouble before?"

"Yes sir." Danny sees Mr. Nowell nod.

"What for?"

"Borrowin' stuff, and skippin' school."

"So you went straight to the Nowells from here?"

"Yes sir."

"Talk to anyone, tell them about the lady?"

Danny shakes his head. Tears burn his eyes. *He don't like me,* Danny moogles. *He don't like foster kids. He'll blame everythin' bad that happens on me.*

"You okay?" Mr. Nowell touches Danny's shoulder.

"I don't like it here," Danny sobs. "I don't remember. I didn't do it!"

"Of course you didn't, the sheriff's just doing his job." They watch the sheriff walk about the grove, bend over, pick up something and put it in a bag.

It's nine o'clock on the patrol car's clock when Mr. Nowell and Danny crawl into the sheriff's car. They share the back seat and ride back to the river in silence. The only sound is the tapping of Danny's heels as his legs jiggle.

They wait for the sheriff to get out of the car and open the door. Mr. Nowell puts his arm around Danny's shoulder.

"Good night," VanOort says, climbing back into his car. "Thanks for you help. I'll be in touch."

Mr. Nowell sighs as he pats Danny's shoulder. They watch the sheriff back out of the driveway, his tires crunching gravel. From the woods, south of the house, they hear a "caha".

"Sounds like someone needs you," Mr. Nowell says.

Owl Rite

VanOort's red tail lights disappear. The moon reflects a silver beam across the Mississippi River.

"We called it a bomber's moon," Mr. Nowell says. He doesn't add, when he was a marine, but Danny knows. "On a night like this you can see everything. The moon shines so bright it hides the stars." He gestures to the sky.

They walk to the stable together. Danny's traps hold two mice. He puts them in a pail and they head back to the house. Mr. Nowell disappears through the backdoor, and Danny puts on his green and tan Mississippi boots. He heads around the house to the river bank, sure of his steps as he passes the honeysuckle bushes that grow under his bedroom window. He pauses at the crest of the river bank and looks out over the shimmering water. Yellow house lights glow from the Wisconsin bluffs. His green dragon hides in the darkness. He hears the sounds of fish splashing as they jump for the mayflies. Crickets chirp and frogs zing. He pees and exhales deeply. *The sheriff's visit is over. Sky Star is buried, the old woman died, Anne ratted and blew my cover. VanOort knows I'm JD and now he'll be watchin' me.* He sniffs the smells of the night. Mayflies smell like fish. The orange tiger lilies and purple vetch share their fragrance. The bushel baskets covering the turtle nursery make eerie shadows. *The Nowells is the longest place I've stayed since Hamm. Has VanOort changed that? When will I need to run?*

He remembers his first night at the Nowells. *Fell down the hill, landed in poison ivy and got all muddy. Mr. Nowell found a pellet under the owl's tree. Put it in my hand and told me owls don't poop. They regurgitate. Nearly threw up holdin' bits of mouse bones and fur. But, by the third night, the owl knew me. Couldn't run then, and can't run now. The owl still needs me.*

He heads down the path. The gray horn sits on a tree branch waiting, an arrogant silhouette in the moonlight. Danny kicks through the dinosaur grass, reed like stalks about two feet tall. Mr. Nowell says the grass grew there with the ancients. Danny shakes the pail and dumps two dead mice onto a nearby tree stump. He sings:

> Owl bird up so high
> Waitin' for your dinner man
> You, me, foster kids

He steps closer, lifts his head and "cahas" The owl "cahas" back.

"So, when you gonna learn to hoot?" Danny teases. "But it's okay. You'll hoot someday, when it's your time to pro cre ate." He stretches out the syllables. "I hope you're a guy, 'cause only guys should hoot for sex." He laughs, stomps his boots in the soft, decaying, mucky leaves under the owl's tree. He pulls his shoulders back, flaps his elbows, and humps the air. He recalls dancing with Anne on Sky Star's grave before they found the dead lady. He remembers Anne pouring water on her shirt and a quick shiver races through his body. *Geeze, why is it everythin' on the river seems like sex? Or death,* he moogles as an afterthought.

BE A MAN

THE NEXT MORNING Anne sweeps through the Nowell's back door, patting her wind-blown hair smooth. She wears a red T-shirt, blue jeans and white Nikes.

"Geeze, what's the big deal?" Danny spoons raspberry syrup on his breakfast waffle.

"Want some breakfast?" Mrs. Nowell motions Anne to sit down. Mr. Nowell pulls out a chair and Anne sits down facing Danny.

"I came to tell you." Her cheeks shine, she gasps to catch her breath. "When the sheriff took me back to the dead lady, her purse was gone." Anne pauses like a dramatic actress. "Someone watched us. We were close to a killer and I'm scared."

"What do ya mean, the old lady's purse was gone?" Danny chokes on a bite of waffle.

"That's what I said. The old lady's purse was gone. The sheriff and me, we found her leaning against the tree with her mouth open and eyes dead, her shoes beside her, her hands in her lap, but no purse." She draws out the word purse like a TV announcer.

"So, that's why VanOort asked about the purse." Danny looks at Mr. Nowell. "He thinks I took the purse."

Mr. Nowell grunts and shrugs his shoulders.

"Well, did you?" Anne demands. Both Nowells look at Anne and then at Danny.

"No way. Do ya think I'd go back?" His voice is loud, almost a shout. His body stiffens.

"Well, I didn't know. Maybe for cigarettes." She shrugs and shakes her head.

Geeze, she thinks she knows everything about me.

Mrs. Nowell puts a glass of orange juice in front of Anne. "Let me fix you a waffle?"

"No thank you, Mrs. Nowell, I'm too upset."

"Of course you're upset," Mr. Nowell agrees. "Finding a body is scary and having to go to the sheriff alone…Danny owes you an apology." He scowls at Danny.

"An apology? For what?" Danny plants his heels under his chair and scrunches his nose.

"For leaving Anne. You certainly didn't act like a man—leaving Anne to do the hard part."

"You wouldn't be a suspect, if you'd come with me." Anne gives him her '*you're so stupid*' stare.

"What do you mean?" Danny barks. He wipes his mouth on his shirt sleeve. "Suspect?"

"Well, if you'd been with me, I'd have known you didn't touch the purse."

"Well I didn't. I couldn't even tell the sheriff what it looked like."

Anne flips her shoulder at him, and her stare implies he's not only stupid but a coward.

She has to be right
Makes me out like I'm guilty
She thinks I'm stupid

"You were brave." Mr. Nowell looks at Anne. "Danny should have gone with you."

Danny's thoughts scream, *Shoud'a, shoud'a, shoud'a. Why is it that everyone wants to tell me what I should do?* He finishes his waffle, slides his chair back and leaves, slamming the back door.

He stomps to the stable. Anne catches up, matching him step for step.

He feeds the horses, giving Yago an extra scoop of oats. Anne leans on Yago's stall door and watches silently. He scrapes up the fresh, green manure in each stall and checks his mice traps. He waits until the horses have licked the last of their oats from the corners of their feed boxes and shoos them out to pasture. He cleans the soles of his shoes on the barn threshold and slams the door shut.

Anne watches and finally says, "I think we should go back and look for the purse."

"And, I'll get Mr. Nowell's spade," Danny agrees.

They bike past the old Bauer Farm taking a short-cut off CR 24. Danny sees no snappers chugging on the shoulder and no crushed mommas on the road. They head south on Highway 61. Cars whiz by them going eighty miles an hour and an Amtrak train zips past on the railroad track next to the north-bound lane.

"How many times have you passed these trees and really seen them?" Anne asks, wheeling into the grove. She leans her bike against a burr oak. The groove chatters with morning noises, a cardinal's wolf-whistle, a wren's song and a woodpecker pecking out a Morse code.

"The yellow tape is gone." Anne indicates a wide circle.

"Here last night." Danny shrugs. "That's where the dead lady sat." He points to a red oak scanning the scene with his Samurai eyes. "There's where we buried Sky Star."

"Let's walk the site," suggests Anne, "like in the movies, but together." She reaches for his hand.

"Okay, what are we lookin' for?"

"I don't know. We'll know when we see it."

They walk a wide circle around trees then a second circle inside the scrub. They walk still smaller circles, going around and around, until they stand by Sky Star's grave.

"Where do we go from here?" Danny faces her and puts his hands on her shoulders.

"What do they look for in the movies?"

"Clues."

"The purse?"

"Footprints?"

"Well, we didn't find a purse," Anne says. "But Danny, look here." She points to the grave site. "Do you remember burying Sky Star?"

"Of course." He doesn't add stupid.

"And what did we do after you covered her grave?"

"I left, I guess."

"I mean before that? Think! You covered her with sand and then what?" She puts her hands on her hips and hops.

Danny frowns. He hates guessing games. *Why can't she just say what she's thinkin'?*

"What did we do after you covered the grave?" She motions her fingers toward her body, coaxing him to think.

"I left."

"No you didn't." She hops again. "We danced. And, what shoes were you wearing?"

"My tennies."

"Well, look at this." She points to the turtle's grave. "Those are boot marks. Boots. Big prints made by a big man."

"Huh?" Danny looks closer. *I shoud'a seen.*

"And where's the shovel?" she asks.

"The spade," Danny corrects. "I put it there." He points to a nearby oak. "Huh?" He circles around and between the trees, and kicks away the leaves on the ground. No spade. He kneels and searches under the buckthorns, sumacs and young oaks ringing the grove. *Had it when I saw the dead lady*, he moogles. "It's gone," he says. He stands up and brushes his pants.

"What are we going to do?" Anne says.

"About the spade?" Danny sighs and shrugs his shoulders. "Mr. Nowell's spade?"

"About the shovel and the boot prints." Anne sighs and gives him her '*you're so stupid*' look. "I think we better see the sheriff. The plot thickens!" She shimmies and Danny watches her breasts jiggle beneath her T-shirt.

"I ain't gonna see no sheriff," Danny protests. "You ain't never been in jail. I have and for nothin'!" *Nothin' being cigarettes, apples and bananas. Now it'll be a damn purse or a spade.* "VanOort don't like me. Once they know you're JD, you're bad, you ain't gotta chance."

"They?"

"The law." He moves toward his bike.

"Don't be silly," she grabs his hand. "We'll go now. Don't make me go alone."

Danny hears Mr. Nowell accusation echo in his thoughts. "*Be a man.*"

THE MISSING PURSE

VanOort sits at his desk reading papers from a file folder, his legs up, his spit-shined shoes resting on his desk. He sees Danny and Anne through the door and stands to greet them.

"Good morning," he says. "Working so early?"

"We went back to the turtle grave this morning," Anne begins.

"To get my dad's spade." Danny clears his throat. "Mr. Nowell's. Borrowed it to bury Sky Star." The word 'borrowed' scratches his throat like a piece of toast gone down wrong.

"But we didn't find it. It's gone," Anne says.

"Oh." The sheriff motions them to sit, pointing to wooden chairs against his office wall.

"We identified the lady, a Mrs. Chester. Lived up Snake Creek Valley Road. Did housekeeping for a family on Sand Prairie. Died of a heart attack, according to the coroner. Had a history of heart problems. Was waiting for a ride, so her husband said when he came to pick her up. We were there with the ambulance."

"So she wasn't murdered?" Anne sighs. "I'm so glad." She blushes. "I mean, I'm sorry she died, but I thought we were close to a murderer. I was scared."

"We don't have many murderers around here, but we still need a sheriff," he reassures her. "I went out this morning and cleared away the crime scene tape, but the woman's purse is missing."

He sits down and puts his feet on the desk again. "So about the spade?"

"It has a green mark," Danny says. "Mr. Nowell marks all his tools to keep them from being borrowed. I left it when I saw the dead lady. It's not there now."

"And besides," Anne begins, "Sky Star's grave has boot prints. Big boot prints." She holds out her hands to measure the size of the boots, her eyes wide with amazement.

"Sky Star? Oh, the turtle." VanOort nods as he remembers.

"When we finished burying Star, we sort of stomped on the grave," Danny explains. "To keep out the critters, like possum and skunks, ya know?"

"We danced," Anne adds, "and now there's these boot prints."

The sheriff sits up, leans forward and rests his elbows on his desk. "We better check that out." He picks up his phone and quickly a woman in a khaki uniform walks through the door. Her blond hair is caught up in a pony tail. She shakes hands with Anne and Danny. She smells like Jenny and Hamm soap. VanOort introduces Abbie Mae, his deputy.

Soon, the four are back at the oak grove. This time the sheriff doesn't turn on the flashing lights when he parks the patrol car, but Danny doesn't like the spooky feeling of being locked in a car with no inside door handles. His legs jiggle as he waits for VanOort to open the back door. Then he, VanOort and Abbie Mae follow Anne to the turtle's grave. She points to the boot marks.

Abbie Mae gets a black bag out of the car and makes casts of the foot prints. When she finishes the sheriff says, "Better dig it up." She gets a shovel out of the car's trunk and uncovers the turtle.

"Glad you didn't bury her deep," she says and smiles at Danny. "But look what we have."

The deputy lifts the carapace up and puts it to the side of the grave. Then she pulls up the purse.

"The purse," Anne gulps.

"The purse," repeats the sheriff. He lifts it up and looks inside. "Interesting. Mr. Chester said his wife had just been paid. Had a couple of hundred dollars, her medication, her driver's license, and a couple of credit cards. Looks like we got a robbery." Danny feels the sheriff's laser stare burn through him.

Abbie Mae puts the purse in a large, plastic bag. "We'll send it off to the state for finger prints," she says, as they walk back to the patrol car.

"You kids did a good job," the sheriff says. "A really good job, cause you didn't mess up the evidence. We have fingerprints and boot casts. We need to work together to stay safe. Maybe some day you'll be a sheriff." He pats Anne's shoulder. "Young lady, you've a keen eye."

Danny scratches his chin.

GOAT PRAIRIE

LATER IN THE morning, Danny and Anne sit on a downed log by Sky Star's grave site. Two black squirrels play tag, running up and down trees and jumping high in the branches. A train whizzes by shrilling out a warning. Cars race by on Highway 61.

"No shovel," Anne says, with a sigh.

"Spade," Danny sighs. *She can't get it right.* He rests his elbows on his knees. They have walked the grove again looking for clues.

"Have you ever been to Snake Creek?" Anne stands.

"Where the dead woman lived?"

"South of Kellogg. Use to be Dakota land. My dad took me there, wanted me to know about my history. Once this whole valley belonged to the Dakotas, before the white man came. Then the government made it a half-breed tract." She waves her arms wide. "I'll show you."

They bike south and turn west onto the Snake Creek Valley Road. Yellow signs with black curvy arrows warn drivers to slow down.

The road's rising grade makes pedaling hard. The gravel road twists between snarls of scrub: sumac, young oak trees, honeysuckle and buckthorn. In some places tall oaks and birch touch their branches across the road and make a shadowy canopy. In other places, the sun shines through the branches making lacy patterns on the gravel. South of the road, a bluff rises hundreds of feet. The north side of the road slides into a deep, dark and swampy ravine that hides the creek. They pass two houses with long driveways built over culverts to guide the spring rains. Every house has a wood pile.

A mile from the highway, far enough to muffle the sound of traffic, they reach a turn-around spot in the road. The creek has moved through a culvert to the south side of the road. On the north, a steep bluff rises to an outcropping of limestone rock. Danny stops to rest. Anne pulls out a bottle of water, takes a long swig, then passes the bottle to Danny. He drinks, leaving some for her to pour on her shirt. She doesn't.

Further down the road, they pass a third house set at the foot of the bluff. The house needs paint. They keep pedaling, the road rising with every twist. The trees give way to green, grassy meadows. Danny's leg muscles go spastic, and he crashes into a ditch. Anne follows, tumbling into the grass beside him, laughing. Danny likes her laugh, gentle, not a sneer like her brother's. Danny rubs his calves. Anne paws through the tall grass. She plucks a slender leaf, puts it between her thumbs and touches it to her lips. She blows and the leaf sings like a reed in her dad's flute.

"Nice," Danny says. He stretches out in the grass. The sky goes up forever.

"There's a goat prairie." Anne points to a bare spot above the smooth outcropping of limestone. "From there we could see the whole Mississippi River flyway."

"A goat prairie? Why is it called a goat prairie?"

"Cause it helps to be a goat to get there," Anne teases. "Not much grows there, grass and brush, stuff only goats eat." She stands, smooths her hips, then reaches for his hand.

"Wanna see?"

Danny flexes his calf muscles and lets her pull him up.

"First," Anne says, "we need walking sticks to make the climb and to scare away the rattlesnakes."

"Rattlesnakes," Danny says. *Walter used a stick to scare away the snakes when we hunted mushrooms.*

Anne walks to a nearby thicket of scrub and brings back two buckthorn branches. She cuts off the prickly sprigs on one stick using a jack knife she carries in her pocket. Danny is amazed and envious.

"That's a real knife," he says.

"Of course," Anne answers. "Did you think I was going to Sky Star's grave unarmed, with maybe a murderer nearby?"

Danny had asked for a knife, but Jenny said *"no"*.

When Anne feels her stick is smooth, she leans on it to test its strength. She then cleans the second branch for Danny.

They climb the bluff, weaving through the knee-high grass that gives way to a sparse covering of weeds holding tight in the sand. They step over fallen rocks washed off the bluff by heavy rains. Danny leans forward on his walking stick, bent like a humped-back old man.

"There's no path," he complains. He groans with each step. A deerfly buzzes his ears. He waves his arm to chase it away. It persists.

Anne reaches the goat prairie first, a level space as smooth and as big as the softball diamond behind their high school. An outcropping of rocks sits behind home plate like a row of front seats. Tiny, button-sized flowers, white and yellow, grow between spindly clumps of brown grass. Wild, pink roses grow along the edge the prairie, where there is dirt.

Danny walks across the sandy diamond toward the rock ledge. He swishes his stick in long sweeps and watches for movement, listening for rattles, being Samurai cautious. He climbs over the boulders, sits down and kicks his legs out into space. Anne sits beside him. They lean their walking sticks beside them.

They look east, toward the Mississippi River. A hundred little green islands appear to float in the water. A white tug pushes a fleet of barges. Danny spies his green dragon along the horizon, resting on a Wisconsin bluff. A smoke stack towers above the

Buffalo power plant at Alma. Huge cumulus clouds sail like heaps of cotton balls in the blue sky. To the south, Anne points out a high ridge of trees.

"Rattlesnake Ridge."

"That why they call this Snake Creek Valley?" Danny asks.

"Lots of rattlesnakes, my dad says."

"So, once this was all Dakota land?" Danny sweeps his arm across the horizon, up and down, then turns south, pointing towards the creek that twists and turns like a snake through the valley.

"That's what my dad says." Anne's tucked a yellow flower behind her ear. She spreads her fingers out on the rocks beside her, leans back and swings her feet.

DAKOTA MEMORIES

"This was Wapasha land. Then, Wapasha land became Wahbasha Village and finally Wabasha. I don't know why or how," Anne begins. "Wapasha was the first of many great Dakota chiefs. Wapasha means red leaf."

"Like red oak or sumac in the fall?" Danny asks.

She shrugs her shoulders.

"The Dakota were driven here, down from the north by other Indians, and then the white man came, *Wasicu*. He brought small pox to the river and many Dakota died."

"The Wasicu wanted our land, thought we were lazy because we didn't farm. We didn't need farms, we hunted and fished. The Wasicu said the Dakota were illiterate and dirty, didn't wash our dishes. We ate mostly with our hands." She mimics eating with her fingers, holding a palm up and twitching her fingers. "We didn't use dishes."

"The Wasicu cut down trees, hunted furs, and plowed the land or what the Indians cried, *"they wounded our mother"*. Finally, the whites bought the land for beads and whiskey, and the government made many treaties." She talks quietly. Danny feels her anger. "But many Dakota didn't leave the river, anyway, for a while."

"You mean, they didn't break cover," Danny says in agreement. *Something Mr. Nowell would say.*

"So, the government set aside land for them, along the river, fifteen miles wide from Red Wing to south of here. Called it a half-breed tract, a land for the children of mixed marriages, French and Dakotas, like my grandpa's pa." She points south towards Rattle Snake Ridge. "But the half-breed strip didn't work. Whites still took the land for farms."

"Then there was a great war west of here. The Indians lost, but many Wasicu died. And, afterwards…." Anne stops and takes a deep breath. "The government sent soldiers. Many Sioux were taken prisoner, some hung. Governor Ramsey said he didn't want any Sioux in Minnesota. So, the soldiers took the Dakotas who lived along the river, loaded them in crates and shipped them down the Mississippi to where it meets the Missouri, then up to Crow River. There many Dakotas starved and died."

Danny wants to reach out and touch her hand. Instead, he kicks his heel against the outcropping and watches the loose rocks fly, landing hundreds of feet below, spraying out like buckshot.

"That's what my dad told me." Anne pulls her legs under her and stands on the ledge. "Once, this was Dakota." She waves her arms wide as if to hold the sky. Danny sees her become an Indian princess. He imagines her hair, long and black, blowing in the gentle breeze. She wears a deer-skin dress and beaded moccasins. *Today, she is Dakota, but last Memorial Day, she was American.* He remembers her poem:

What can I be?
What do I want to be?
What will I be?

I can be a daughter
I want to be a Dakota daughter
I will be a daughter who fights for equality

I can be an American
I want to be strong and do my part
I will pledge my troth to stand brave for those who died for me.

Her poem won first prize. He and Walter were proud of her. They coached her to recite her poem for the program. He smiles to himself, remembering his argument, *'troth is a girl word.'*

Standing on the ledge, Danny dusts his backside with a quick pat. He tousles Anne's hair, catches her around the waist and draws her close. He kisses a tear on her wet cheek and tastes the salt. She blushes and starts to pull away. He grabs her hand.

"Damn!" he says. "I'm sorry." She leans her cheek against his shoulder and sobs a hiccup. A gentle breeze sweeps by them.

"It makes me sad," she says. She waves her hand toward the valley. "I'm most sad because I can never be all Dakota. I'm just a half-breed." A shadow rushes over them. He elbows Anne's ribs to look up.

"Turkey vulture," Danny sees the short neck, thin line of wing and finger-like wing tips. They watch the bird rise, silently lifting its body upwards on a chimney thermo until it disappears into the blue sky. "I think your Dakotas heard you."

"You think so?" She hiccups again. "Strange. My Dad married my mom, a Lakota from Crow River, then, he moved back here. I guess the river drew him like it did the Dakotas before him."

Danny and Anne hold hands and look again at the panoramic view of the Mississippi River flyway. After a while, they turn westward.

"Look!" Anne points to line fences that marked where there'd been fields. She points to a zigzag path. "A deer trail, probably leads to water, or it's a cow trail that leads to that clearing. See the footings of the old barn? See?" And then they see the tent. "Wonder who camps there?" she says.

Camp Site

"LET'S FIND OUT." Danny picks up his walking stick, and crosses the goat prairie while sweeping a path before him. "No snakes," he calls.

"There's got to be a path down," Anne insists. She circles the edge of the goat prairie, and sweeps the grasses with her stick. She finds a path. They leave the goat prairie and dig their sticks into the dirt alongside the path to keep from falling. Danny feels a stirring of excitement in his belly. *I'm Samurai.*

> *We will discover*
> *Who lives on the old homestead*
> *Be he friend or foe*

The trail ends near the old barn footings. The tent site is quiet. Danny holds his hand over the fire pit ashes. "Cold."

Nearby, a stack of wood is piled neatly. There's a folding camp chair, and a tin of crackers with a bucket of water on a small table. Boot prints and dog tracks carpet the area. A towel hangs on a nearby bush. A few feet away, through a stand of birch and oak trees, the sound of Snake Creek rushes by.

"Anyone here?" Danny calls, waits, then, calls again.

"This is someone's place," Anne says. "We shouldn't trespass."

"Trespass? Geeze, we ain't gonna hurt nothin'," Danny protests. "Maybe this is an Indian guy."

"I don't like being here," Anne argues. "Let's go." She points to tire tracks by the old barn and motions Danny to follow. Danny hesitates. *What if we found a dead guy here and this was a crime scene? What would I tell VanOort? Think Samurai: Where are you? What do you see? What do you hear? What do you want to happen?*

He answers himself. *I'm below a goat prairie in Snake Creek Valley, near what was once a barn. I hear water and I want to know who lives here.*

Anne hollers from the road, "Come on."

And I'm not scared like some dumb female.

Danny grunts. He navigates the tire ruts to where Anne waits. They find their bikes, and she leads the way down the steep winding road. As they approach Highway 61, they brake as a van painted in green and brown camouflage colors turns onto Snake Creek Valley Road. The driver stops, leans out the window and spits. He wears dark shades and a beret that matches his van.

"What you kids up to?" he growls.

"Nothin'," Danny answers. "Biked up the road, hiked the bluff."

The van guy spits again. "Mess around by my camp?"

"No," Anne answers. "You live there, in that tent?"

"I got government permission. Just stay away, ya hear. Don't need no nosy kids hangin' round." He revs the van's motor and spins the wheels kicking up a spray of gravel.

Danny and Anne watch him go. Anne shrugs her shoulders.

"Not a friendly Indian," Danny teases. "I like you better."

"I hope so. Anyway, he's gotta be Norwegian, with a yellow beard."

Geeze, Danny moogles. *Why is it? She sees everythin'.*

RIVER KILL

"YOU'RE A VERY good cook." Danny flashes Mrs. Nowell one of his charming smiles and finishes a second helping of strawberry shortcake piled high with whipped cream. She chuckles and clears the table. Mr. Nowell nurses his second cup of coffee and reads the local newspaper, a weekly that comes out on Tuesday.

"There's a meeting in Lake City tonight." He puts down the paper and looks at his wife. "Something about a pumped storage project, with a power company and FERC, the Federal Energy Regulatory Commission." He folds the paper on his lap. "Never know what the government plans to do," he says. "Last year they wanted to cut down all the trees in our backyard to dump dredged sand in a pile ten feet tall. It took a sharp guy to figure out their own laws prohibit dumping sand so near the river. They must stay back from the water a thousand feet." Mr. Nowell grunts deep in his belly. "Danny, how'd you like to come with me? This may be important."

Danny nods yes and heads for the bathroom to slick down his hair. *The man wants me to come with him, like I'm really part of the family.*

Mr. Nowell heads the truck north to Lake City. Danny watches his driving process, pressing the clutch, shifting gears and easing the gas pedal as they turn onto Highway 61. At Reads Landing, Mr. Nowell slows the truck to fifty miles-an-hour.

"Did you know that once Reads was a booming river town with thirty bars and that many hotels?" he asks.

Danny nods. He learned that Reads was even considered to be the capitol of Minnesota.

"But things change, and change changes things," Mr. Nowell says. He scratches his eyebrow. "After the trappers took all the beaver and muskrats from around here, Reads became a logging town. The loggers harvested Wisconsin's virgin forests and floated the trees down the Chippewa. At Reads, they maneuvered the logs downstream on the Mississippi to saw mills at Winona, LaCrosse, and Dubuque. There are pictures in the library of log jams, where the river is solid wood."

Danny smiles to himself. *The old man says virgin like it ain't a sex word.*

"Reads was a rowdy place. Some folks say there were at least a couple of murders every week."

"Geeze."

"Then, after the lumber barons, like Andrew Tainter, the Bull of the Woods, made their millions and the trees were gone, logging stopped. Reads died. No hotels, no saloons, no customers. The railroad laid tracks alongside the river and the Corp of Engineers built Lock and Dam #4 in Alma. That backed up the river for forty miles, flooded much of Reads, and low land farms and woods close to the river. Today, Reads is one street, three blocks long beside the river, with a bunch of houses built on a river bluff."

"Here today, gone tomorrow." Danny taps his feet on the truck's floorboard. He's heard the words somewhere, but can't remember where.

"True." Mr. Nowell looks at Danny and smiles. "When did you get so philosophical?"

"Huh?"

At the Lake City High School, they join the throng shoving into the auditorium to find seats. People greet Mr. Nowell, including Sheriff VanOort, who is out of uniform. He shakes Danny's hand and asks how things are going. Danny mumbles "okay." The sheriff sits in the row behind them. Danny squirms feeling watched. *This sheriff is really dangerous,* he moogles.

On the stage, people cluster in small groups. Mr. Nowell calls them government people. Some wear green shirts and pants with badges on their sleeves.

A man blows into the microphone to get attention, then, he greets the crowd. He introduces all the guys on stage. Another guy explains the power company's proposal to build a pumped storage. The company would pump water from Lake Pepin to the top of a bluff six miles south of Lake City. The water would be held in a reservoir and released for high energy usage. The power company plans to sell the energy to neighboring states. Pumping the water up the bluff would cause the level of Lake Pepin to fluctuate twice a day. Mr. Nowell grunts.

"What's fluctuate?" Danny whispers.

Mr. Nowell raises and lowers his hand.

"Oh."

Another man, wearing khaki pants, says he doesn't favor the proposal, but says the state can't stop it because FERC is a federal authority. Mr. Nowell groans. He leans forward in his seat and holds his head as if he's got toothaches on both sides of his jaw.

When the government people ask for questions, Mr. Nowell stands up. "If the level of the lake goes up and down twice a day, how will that affect water levels downriver?"

"They'll go up and down, too," the DNR man says with a nod.

"What will that do to the river life? Beaver? Muskrats? Birds? All the nesting areas?" Mr. Nowell waits for an answer.

"Won't be good," the DNR man answers. Mr. Nowell sits down. He clenches his fists. His knuckles turn white. VanOort pats his shoulder.

Other people stand and ask questions. Each answer makes the crowd murmur, rumblings like thunder harkening a storm. The men on the stage agree the pumped storage project is a bad idea, and say they are against it. This news makes the people in the auditorium clap. Mr. Nowell slides lower in his seat. "Fools," he mumbles. "Can't they hear? FERC is a federal authority."

When the meeting is over, Mr. Nowell stops at the door and talks to a small group of people. "It's wrong, don't they understand?" he asks. "The state can't stop the pumped storage project."

"Who can?" The man wears leather boots laced to his knees.

"We can!" exclaims a woman. "And, if we don't, they'll kill our river."

"What can we do?" chimes in another woman. She stands next to a tall man with a puffy cap of silver-gray hair.

"We need a meeting," Mr. Nowell says, "tomorrow night."

"Meet at my store," says the man wearing the boots, "Jeff's Bargain Hunter. I'll open the door at seven. I'll even make coffee. Will someone bring cookies?"

Danny and Mr. Nowell return to the truck.

"Will the pumped storage make all the baby birds on the river die?" Danny asks after he slams the truck door and buckles his seatbelt.

Mr. Nowell shakes his head and doesn't answer. Danny feels the silence is a *"yes"*, a bad thing. Guilty feelings creep inside him. *My dad didn't talk when he was angry, and I guess Mr. Nowell is angry.* Danny slumps down, leans against the truck's door and clicks the lock button. *I like it better when people yell.*

Mr. Nowell revs the motor. "You were right, Danny boy. Here today, gone tomorrow." He spins the tires as they leave the parking lot.

Danny wants to ask a hundred questions. *How will the pumped storage hurt the beavers and the muskrats? Will pumping water up the bluff kill all the fish? Will the birds and animals be like the Dakotas? Lose their homes to what the white man wants? Who can stop the pumped storage project? Whose side is the government on?*

PUMPED STORAGE

On Wednesday, the next night, on their way to Lake City, Mr. Nowell passes the sheriff's car parked behind a van painted in camouflage colors.

"Talked to VanOort lately?" Mr. Nowell asks.

"Nah!" Danny braces his feet against the truck's floor. He stares out the window.

"Thought he might."

"What?"

"Talk to you."

"Why?" *Does Nowell think I'm guilty?* Danny feels a heavy mood invade the truck. *There are two guys I don't wanna see, VanOort and the Norwegian.*

Mr. Nowell is quiet and looks straight ahead. A few minutes north of Reads, he points to a lone eagle soaring over the Mississippi River.

"Hundreds of eagles winter here. This is where the Chippewa dumps into the Mississippi and keeps the water stirred up. The river rarely freezes, a condition called confluence." The man points toward Wisconsin. "There's Pepin. Once had a big fish factory. When I was a kid like you, they paid me a nickel a fish." He smiles as his thoughts warm a secret place deep inside him. Next, he points to the town of Stockholm.

"Settled by Swedes." Mr. Nowell laughs. "They hold a big

77

reunion in the park. People come from Sweden and act out the story of their relatives coming to America. They tell how one fellow organized the move with lots of promises, then takes everyone's money. At the reunion, they sing Swedish songs, but the part I like best is when the trains come by and blast their horns at the park's crossing. Everyone on the stage stops, mid-song or sentence, then start up right where they were before the train. Never miss a beat."

"Like a commercial?" Danny asks. Mr. Nowell nods and points across the river to the town of Maiden Rock.

"Heard about Maiden Rock?" he asks.

"Anne told me. An Indian girl jumped off a cliff. Drowned 'cause her dad, the chief, wouldn't let her marry the guy she loved." *Dumb.*

Further north on 61, Mr. Nowell points again to Wisconsin. "Fort Antoine. Built by the French long before Minnesota became a state. The French were fur traders and they married Indian women, often the chiefs' daughters. Got better furs that way. Their children were called half-breeds. Our river's history goes way back."

Danny nods.

Inside Lake City's city limits, Mr. Nowell slows and parks in front of *Jeff's Bargain Hunter*. Danny steps through the door and listens to the floor squeak. He looks around. Shiny tin ceiling tiles reflect the stores' lights. A stag head, with an antler spread of twelve boards, hangs on the wall. Jeff, wearing his laced up boots, greets them and shakes their hands. The store smells of old stuff.

Soon, others arrive. Jeff sets out the coffee pot and a tray of mismatched mugs. "Don't use Styrofoam. Not river friendly."

Danny selects a cup decorated with a crowing rooster, fills it half full with hot, black coffee and adds cream and sugar up to the rim. An older woman opens a box of chocolate chip cookies. The smell makes Danny's mouth water. He takes two.

Jeff has set out rickety metal chairs. The Cookie Lady, who Danny recognizes from the pumped storage meeting, has a farm on top of the bluff, near where the power company plans to put the reservoir. She grows blueberries, raspberries, and apples. She invites everyone to visit her farm.

Another lady, dressed in an aqua dress with a wooden necklace shaped in the form of an anchor, says she's a boat lady. She lives in a town eighty miles west, but docks her sailboat in Lake City's marina.

The man with puffy white hair lives on the shore of Lake Pepin. He calls his wife, Honeydo. He has a radio program and tells people what's happening on the river. "Next week, Lake City will have its annual Water Skiing Festival. Lake City is the birthplace of water skiing," he says. His name is George. Her name is Helen.

Helen Honeydo, tells how Lake Pepin got its name. When a Father Hennepin explored the upper Mississippi River before Minnesota became a state, he saw Sioux warriors mourning for one of their dead on the lake shore. He called the site "Lac de Pleurs, a "Lake of Tears." After Helen finishes her story, she chokes and wiggles her chair. "If we don't stop that—that—that pumped storage, we'll all be crying in a Lake of Tears." Her face turns red. Her husband pats her hand and coos, "Honeydo, calm down."

Mr. Nowell introduces Danny. "We live on the river," he says. "Downstream. If the water fluctuates every day, all the birds' nests and the muskrat and beaver homes near us will be destroyed."

"Oh no," Honeydo Helen sighs and holds her head.

"We need to do something," Jeff says. "We need to get organized." He slaps his knee.

"We need a name," Honeydo George says, "a fighting name." He jabs his fists in the air.

"Concerned Citizens Against the Pumped Storage Project," the Boat Lady suggests.

Jeff suggests shortening it to C-CAPS.

A good name is Crow, Danny moogles. *We heard the alarm, now we attack.* He pounds his knee with a fist.

"C-CAPS," Mr. Nowell says, "I like the way it sounds."

Honeydo George repeats, "C-CAPS," using his radio voice. His wife nods and smiles.

"We need more people," Jeff adds. "Invite everyone we know to our next meeting. We need many voices to save our river."

The Boat Lady promises to send out notices to all the local papers.

The group lists all the newspapers to contact. They agree to call themselves *"C-CAPS".*

"Oh dear," Honeydo Helen says. "I fear we're like the Sioux crying on the banks of Lac de Pleurs."

"But we're not dead," Honeydo George says.

"Newspaper ads cost money," says the Cookie Lady. "I know, I advertise when my blueberries and raspberries need picking."

Quickly, the group agrees to contribute a hundred dollars each. Danny watches Mr. Nowell open his wallet. He looks at Danny, raises his eyebrows in a questioning way, and gives Jeff two hundred-dollar bills.

Danny moogles, *Wow!*

On the way home, Danny and Mr. Nowell talk about the meeting.

"I think we shoud'a called ourselves Crows," Danny says. "We heard the alarm. Now we need more cheerleaders."

"You've got the right idea," Mr. Nowell says. "And if we're lucky, we'll attract some real attackers."

"Like who?"

"Whom." Mr. Nowell says. "I've some ideas. Like the crows, we need a strategy."

"Are we going to attack the pumped storage like the crows did our owl?"

"Yes. If we can make the project unpopular—or unprofitable—maybe we can get the power company to break cover."

"That would be a pretty, big bird." Danny smiles and imagines a big vulture spiraling up a wind chimney. He snuggles down and looks out the truck's window. The lights from Pepin zip by like jewels in the night. *Mr. Nowell is pretty smart, like a Samurai.*

BE QUIET

AFTER FRIDAY NIGHT's supper, Danny ties Yago to a small oak growing next to the Goulette lodge. The horse whinnies and stomps his front leg. Anne and Walter sit with their dad by a low campfire waiting for the smoke to ward away the mosquitoes. The sun hangs in the western sky casting long shadows.

Danny pets Charlie and then sits on a log near Anne. She offers him a green, willow stick and a marshmallow. A tree frog serenades a mate in the early evening. The river laps its bank with a soothing sound. A barge's blast echoes up the river canyon, chasing some sleepy fisherman out of the main channel. A cicada shrills.

"Have you ever fished for trout?" Walter asks.

"Trout? Nope. Just northerns with you, that's all." Danny sticks his marshmallow in the flame and watches it flare up. He blows out the torchy sweet, pinches off the crisp brown, pops it into his mouth, and sucks his thumb with a loud smack. "What's the difference? Fishin' trout?"

"You have to shut up." Walter flashes his know-it-all smile. "Bet you can't quit talking for a half-hour."

"How much?" Danny likes the challenge, he takes to gambling.

"A dollar an hour."

"An hour? You just said a half-hour."

"Just upped the ante," Walter says. "More challenging."

"You're on. When do we go?"

"Tomorrow, after you practice."

"Practice what?"

"Not talking." Walter grunts and smiles. Danny threads another marshmallow on his willow stick. A long silence hangs around the campfire.

"Geeze." Danny scratches his legs and moans.

"Gotcha! Two minutes." Walter smirks. "Trout fishing is like hunting. You stand tall and silent like a tree. No bright colors. No talking. You point and use hand signs. Sneak up on them like the ancient ones. No vibrations." He points his finger at Danny. "Walk quiet and shut up. No noise, like you throwing a pop can in the water."

"Get off it, will ya?" When fishing northerns, Danny tossed an empty pop can into the river. It annoyed Walter, more than annoyed. Walter reminds him often with lectures on keeping the river clean.

Danny peels off a crust of marshmallow. He sucks the hot, crispy sweetness from his fingers and thrusts the remaining gob over the fire until it bursts in flames. He blows on it quickly. "Where we going?" he asks.

"Snake Creek."

"Snake Creek?" Danny's knees jiggle and the remaining marshmallow falls into the fire. *Geeze, no.*

"But before we go," Walter says, "you need to practice casting." He disappears into the lodge and returns with a rod and reel. He tapes a ping pong ball on the line and shows Danny how to cast. Danny watches. Walter drops the line with his hand, then using a pendulum swing, rocks the rod back and forth. At the peak of the swing, he releases the trigger and lets the line fly.

"Let it go about four or five lengths before you hit the trigger." He shows Danny the trigger. "Then let it drift." Walter executes a great cast. Danny watches the ball zip out and bounce on the grass. Danny takes the rod, holds the line, and Walter talks him through the first try. After several successful practice swings, Danny sets the rod and reel aside.

Walter puts another log on the smoldering embers. Danny grabs a marshmallow and a new stick. He waits for the fire to blaze.

The night has closed around them. Two far away stars shine above a banana moon. Venus and Jupiter hang in the western sky. Drops of water in the firewood sputter. Yago munches grass nearby, and a second voice joins the tree frog song.

Not A Good Day

A FOGGY SATURDAY morning chills Danny's plans to fish trout. He snuggles under the bed covers while his thoughts flicker. *Do I go or not? Should I stay in bed?* He thinks about looking at the girly magazines between his mattress and box spring. Finally, he crawls out of his cozy nest and discovers his favorite Twins shirt and soft blue jeans are in the wash. He settles for the sweat shirt and jeans Mrs. Nowell bought at a garage sale. *At least they're soft.*

Nothing goes right. The mouse traps in the barn are empty. Yago puts on a nicky-fit and Danny steps in a pile of stinky, ripe, steamy-green manure. His breakfast bacon is burned and his scrambled eggs runny. Mrs. Nowell has made cheese sandwiches for his fishing lunch because she forgot to buy peanut butter, and packs in carrots and celery sticks instead of potato chips. As he leaves, he notes his rain slicker is bright yellow. Lastly, to add to his miserable morning, Mr. Nowell suggests Danny wear his ugly, brown and green, rubber Mississippi River boots.

"They squeak," Danny growls.

Mr. Nowell grunts.

Danny bikes into the Goulette lodge site glad the turtle-mission season is over. The morning fog rolls down the river towards Alma, lifting gently as if it is the great wings of a white bird in flight. The river is quiet. No boats. No tree frogs. No mosquitoes. Charlie climbs down the ladder and greets him with a swipe of the tongue. Walter and Anne sit with their dad at the picnic table drinking coffee. Anne pours him a cup. He hugs the warm mug to his chest.

"So you guys are going fishing," Mr. Goulette says. "Where?"

"Snake Creek, for trout," Walter says. Anne snorts and gives Danny a panicky look. Danny puts his finger to his lips.

"So, are you after my Brown at the Bend of the River?" Mr. Goulette's dark eyes twinkle with fun. He stretches his legs, bumps the table and makes his coffee cup wiggle.

"The what?" Danny asks.

"An old trout my dad's been trying to catch for years. They're buddies," Walter uses his know-it-all voice.

"Well, if he happens to bite, put him back. He's mine. Just feed him the water worms." Mr. Goulette chuckles.

"Water worms? What about willowcats?" Danny puzzles. He and Walter caught willowcats to bait northerns. The tiny cats get lots of respect with their 'knock you on your butt' stingers.

"Trout like water worms," Walter says. "Snake Creek's the best place to find them.

Danny looks at Anne. His legs ache. He imagines biking Snake Creek's uphill road toting a backpack, rain slicker and fishing gear.

"We'll get the worms on the way." Walter gulps the last of his coffee and puts on a fishing vest with deep pockets. Anne gives Danny an empty metal can that advertises tea.

"For the worms." She taps the cover and smiles. Coyly.

Outside the lodge, Walter ties the fishing rods and reels onto their bikes with leather shoe strings. Danny reaches for his rain slicker.

"No! No! Can't do." Walter grabs the yellow slicker and flings it to the ground. "If it rains, we'll find a bush." He looks at Danny with an air of authority. Danny groans inside, reminded of the first kid at Hamm who punched him. The first and last time he got cheated at Farkle.

"I'll freeze to death," counters Danny, balling his fists in his jean pockets and containing the urge to deck his friend.

"Naw, you won't."

"Who says?"

"Me." Walter mounts his bike and ends the conversation. Charlie gives them a goodbye bark from his ladder. Danny pedals fast to keep up. Walter is in good shape from football practice. The tin can bounces in Danny's bike's basket. The fishing rods make peddling awkward. He flexes his shoulders to shift his backpack. *This ain't my idea of fun.*

When they pass Sky Star's grave site, Danny expects to see VanOort's patrol car. The sheriff turns up in the most unusual places, and today is not a good day.

> *When you're a JD*
> *The law thinks guilty, guilty*
> *Who buried the purse?*

Spring Hole

THE BLANKET OF gray clouds over Snake Creek Valley holds back its rain. The morning air is chilly. Danny's glad he has worn a sweat shirt. At the Snake Creek Valley Road sign, Walter edges onto the gravel shoulder and stops. Danny follows. They lay their bikes in the damp grass, shift out of their back packs and head down a slippery slope to the creek, stepping over a jumble of logs and branches left by an early spring flood. Walter points to the spring hole.

"See. The center is a lighter color than around the edge, tells me this is a spring hole." Walter talks loud, like he's giving a tour and knows it all.

Danny nods. *Who cares? What stupid guy hears a creek talk?* But then as if on cue, a red-wing black bird scolds their intrusion, cocking his head, giving them an evil eye.

Walter retrieves a rusty window screen and an old rake stashed under a brush pile.

"Get the worm can," he commands.

Danny retrieves the can and retraces his steps to find Walter knee-deep in the creek. The spring hole is clear, the bottom layered with round-tipped, yellow oak leaves. Danny takes off his shoes. The cold water sends a shiver up his backbone that makes his teeth chatter.

Walter rakes the wet leaves off the bottom and dumps them

on the floating screen. He moves his hand across the screen and gently swirls the goo. A black worm, about an inch long, pops out. Walter holds the worm to Danny's nose, eye level.

"See the whiskers? You put the fish hook through the lips." Walter puckers his lips. "If you miss the lips, all his insides gush out and you have a flat worm. Trout don't like flat worms."

Danny nods. *Ish! I didn't like getting stung by willowcats, but these water worms are worse.*

Walter puts the worm, with a handful of leaves, into the can. He rakes up more wet leaves and spreads them across the screen.

"Isn't there an easier way?" Danny grumbles as he helps Walter push the leaves around. "This makes my hands stink."

"To catch trout?"

"No, to get bait."

"Sure. Some fishermen buy spinners or flies, but not me, not my dad." A serious look comes over Walter's face. "You might say water worms are our tradition, we use the ancient ways. Besides, we fish for food, not for sport."

"Oh." *Walter fishes for food. Like me on a run, borrowing tomatoes, kohlrabi or melons. Eating is serious business. The best time to run is now, in summer, when people have gardens. And I guess now, is the best time for fishing.*

When Walter counts twenty worms in the can, he wades out of the pool, sits on a log, and examines his toes. "Checking for blood suckers," he says, spreading his toes apart.

Danny sits beside him and checks his toes. He finds one black, shiny sucker.

"How do you get him off?" He burps and tastes his breakfast eggs.

"Just pull," Walter snaps.

"Won't that hurt?"

"Not me," Walter grins and elbows Danny in the ribs. Danny wiggles his toes. The sucker clings tight.

Danny Malloy, Samurai Summer

Water worms, blood suckers
Shoud'a stayed in bed cause
This fishin' ain't fun

Danny takes a deep breath, yanks, flings the creature into the pool, and wipes his hands on Walter's jeans.

No Talkin'

Walter and Danny bike up Snake Creek Valley road, winding past the goat prairie and the tent site. Danny pedals fast and looks straight ahead. He doesn't want to meet the man who camps there, who drives the brown and green van. *Don't need someone squealin' to VanOort that I've been trespassin'.*

The road twists between birch and pine trees and bumps over a small bridge. To the north, bluffs hide their tops in the blanket of clouds. On the south side, the bluffs slide into a deep ravine cut by flood waters, into a tangle of scrub, downed trees and rocks strewn about by an angry god.

They bike until the road divides a farm yard, the house on one side, the barn and out buildings on the other. An orange and white horse grazes on the steep bluff behind the house. Red cows nap in the barnyard. A few lift their white faces to watch the bikers go by. Beyond the farm, Walter stops at a wide turn-around place. Fields of corn and bean peek through the brush like secret islands in an Irish wood. Someone has planted acres of walnut trees.

Walter shoves his bike under a bush and hides his backpack in the tall grass. He motions Danny to do the same.

"The creek's just over that rise," Walter whispers. "But before we go—" He hands Danny a jar of petroleum jelly. "Tick insurance."

Danny opens the jar and smears the jelly on the bottom of his jeans, just like they did when hunting mushrooms.

"Now, more bug insurance." Walter pulls out a jack knife, a beautiful knife, dark red, fat, with several blades. Like Anne's. Walter snaps open a blade. It's the kind of knife Jenny wouldn't allow.

Walter searches the bushes and cuts two branches, each with three long fingers. "My ancestors used these to keep away the deer flies and the no-see'ems." He twists the two outside fingers of the branch into a halo and puts it on his head. The third finger flops over his head. He helps Danny braid his halo.

They head west, through a stand of tall grass, and a barrier of scrub. Walter eases through the scrub like he's oiled. Danny feels every brush snag his jeans. The thorns scratch his hands. "Wish I'd worn gloves," he grumbles.

Snake Creek runs twelve-feet wide at the bottom of a deep gully. Trees lay on both banks, uprooted by flood waters. Yellow limestone boulders are strewn about.

"Quiet," Walter whispers, "this is the first walk-on-by." He motions Danny to pass the widening of the creek and follow a narrow path. They pass a second and then a third walk-on-by. At a fourth, Walter stops. "Brown at the Bend in the River," he whispers. He squats and stares at the water. Three black fish slide over the rocky creek bed.

"Suckers, stone rollers and a red horse, no trout," Walter whispers. "We'll go on."

They follow the Snake as it tumbles, riffle after riffle, then widens into three pools. A path of rocks make steps through the water to the far side.

"Here's where the hunt begins," Walter whispers. He points up stream. "There's where the trout hide. When they move, sometimes they stir the water up. You need to pay attention."

Danny sighs. Walter makes him feel like he's in school. His head feels funny with the halo bobbing. He feels watched. He tugs Walter's shirt.

"Are there bears here? Or bobcats?" he whispers. "I gotta sneaky feelin' we're bein' watched."

Walter shakes his head and rolls his eyes. "Give me the worms." He pulls out a worm, and points to a spot on the worm's face between wiggling rows of whiskers. "Put the hook there," he whispers. Danny watches, not keen on holding worms, much less hooking worm lips. Walter puts more worms in his pocket.

"If you get a nibble," Walter whispers, "don't yank the line. Let the trout taste it. He'll take the worm up creek, nudge it around a bit and won't really bite till the third time. And remember, no talkin'." He looks at his watch. "Be quiet for one hour." He points to a shelf of land jutting over the creek, a hundred feet upstream. He crosses the creek silently like a trout hunter.

Danny finds a downed log, sits, and contemplates baiting a water worm's lips. He can't shake the feeling he's being watched.

It's an ancient place
Feels like bein' with the dead
Dakotas watchin'

He thinks about Jenny and her Samurai, 'Listening to the Ants'. *Maybe today what I'm hearin' is water worms.* He smiles to himself and rotates his shoulders to ease the tension. His halo bobs.

Upstream, Walter reels in a flopping fish and waves.

Danny waves back and ties a hook on his line using a double knot. He digs for a worm. The first worm slips through his fingers and vanishes into the creek. He grabs a second worm and looks it in the eye. "Whatcha gotta say today?" He cautiously slips the hook through the worm's lips.

He strains to remember everything Walter says about fishin' trout. First, there's pendulum swing. Then hit the trigger and let the worm sink into the creek. Soon, he feels a tug and then another. *I've got a fish.* He pulls his arm back and yanks the fish out of the water. It flaps wildly on the bank, its puckered lips sucking air. He works the hook out of the fish's mouth, and threads a stringer through its gill. He anchors the stringer to a nearby bush. His hands are wet and slimy and he wipes them on his jean pants.

He hooks another water worm's lips and casts out, feeling great to be even with Walter, one fish to one fish. He tries to relax, but the creepy feeling of being watched crawls up his back. He shrugs his shoulders. He scratches his neck. His halo sways. He knows the feeling of being watched, he feels like he's at Speedy's before he got sentenced to Hamm.

Visitor

Time moves slowly, what seems an hour is only ten minutes. Danny dangles the water worm in the creek. Walter moves further upstream, casts his line and flicks it like he's dancing. He catches another fish. Danny moves downstream and climbs out on a tree limb that hangs over a quiet pool. He casts upstream, swaying like a pendulum. He watches his line float past him and hook on a rock. He shakes and wiggles his rod until the hook gives. He casts again and releases the trigger too late. The line catches a bush on the other side of the creek. He whips his rod with a quick wrist action until the hook sails back to him. The worm is gone. He dangles the hook in the creek. *This is the way to fish trout.*

More minutes pass. The cloudy gray sky makes him sleepy, and he closes his eyes. Walter said the clouds make for good fishing, the trout can't see shadows. Danny suddenly wakes with a jerk. A yellow face peeks through the brush from across the creek. Their eyes connect. Danny feels a chill zip through his body. His toes curl. He counts, one minute, two, three. The face disappears, moving the brush with a whisper.

Danny's knees shake. *It's the Norwegian!* Minutes pass, then an animal emerges behind Walter, a large dog, reddish gold, streaked with black, with a narrow nose for rutting rabbits. *That's no dog, it's a coyote.* Danny starts to warn Walter but gulps, *the bet.* He waves his hands in the air. *So, what?*

It's a-no-win win
Yell and scare the dog away
Kiss my buck goodbye

The creature sits on its haunches, statue like, ears alert. Danny rests his elbows on his knees and whispers, "Walter, there's a coyote sitting behind you, but if I tell you out loud, I lose the bet."

The animal stands, stretches and sits again, loose, like he's hinged together. *Maybe that's what's been watching me. It's big.*

Walter reels in his line and casts again. The animal moves its head back and forth in time with Walter's dancing but stays behind him. More minutes pass. The creature stands again, alert and listening. It looks over its shoulder, then like magic, it becomes a squatting man, an old Indian, an ancient one with a pointy chin, black eyes, leathery skin and a knot of hair on the top of his head. The Indian looks toward Danny.

Danny springs to his feet and shakes his head. He rubs his eyes. *Am I sleepin'?* The man stands, backs into the brush, and fades away. The coyote-dog reappears for a moment, then disappears. Danny's insides beat like a base drum. He digs in his pocket for a smoke stick, but there's none. He counts to ten. *It's gotta be the Norwegian guy. Should I tell Walter, but that'd be talkin'.*

Upstream, Walter waves and points to his watch. He holds up his hand and wiggles his fingers. Danny digs out another worm and climbs back onto the oak limb. His hand trembles as he hooks the worm's lips. He casts, and lets the bobber float into the pool beneath him. *Geeze I'm glad the trout ain't bitin'. What do I tell Walter? He* tries to relax and sit quietly.

"You had a coyote watching you," Danny says, as Walter crosses the rock pathway.

"Sure!" Walter sneers.

"Really, a coyote!" Danny pantomimes a long nose and pointy ears.

"If you say so," Walter chuckles. "Why didn't you yell, or something?"

"And lose the bet?" Danny sneers back, sniffing.

Walter gives Danny a playful push and opens his vest. He shows four trout.

"Brookies and browns, the brookies have the yellow sides. Anne can fry them for our supper."

Danny retrieves his fish.

"That's not a trout," Walter laughs. "You caught a sucker, a stone roller."

"It's a fish." Danny argues.

"But not an eatin' fish, too many bones."

Danny can see Walter thinking, *the sucker caught a sucker.*

Walter picks up the stone roller and shakes it off the stringer. He tosses the fish on the creek bank.

"For your coyote," he says.

Danny thrusts his hands in his pockets, if he were at Hamm, he'd punch Walter in the lip.

They ease through the scrub and thread their way through the tall grass to their bikes, mindful of snakes. The halos bounce on their heads. Danny rubs his hands and counts his scratches. "Ten." He thinks about the Norwegian, the coyote, the Indian, and telling Walter. He'd tell Walter, but his friend would only sneer.

They find their bikes, and Walter discovers his backpack is gone.

"Did you sneak back here and hide it?" His voice is angry. He stands with his hands on his hips.

"Nope, not guilty." *Guilty* blurts out so quickly, Danny cringes. The word burns his lips. *Damn VanOort. I'm not guilty. I shoud'a run.*

"Are you sure?" Walter's tone ignites Danny. He thrusts his

hands in his pockets and '*grrs*'. Walter circles the grass and finds a trail of bent grass leading off into the brush. "Something dragged my backpack off. I guess we had a visitor. Guess, I lost one lunch, one knapsack, and one buck." Walter thrusts out his hand to shake Danny's. "A coyote, you say?"

Or something else too
smart for cheese sandwiches
Carrots and celery

Strategies

On Friday evening after bedding the horses down, before the fire flies flirt about with their flashing lights, Danny and Mr. Nowell drive to the second C-CAPS meeting. Danny wears his Twins shirt and matching cap, bought on an outing with the Hamm guys.

At Reads Landing, Mr. Nowell slows to the fifty-mile speed limit and passes VanOort, parked by the road side. Mr. Nowell lifts his pointer finger off the steering wheel and moves it up and down. VanOort gives the same wave back.

Danny slouches in his seat and looks out the window. "VanOort gives me a pain," he whines. "He's a crow. Thinks if he stays in my face, I'll break cover. But I didn't take the old lady's purse."

"Interesting," Mr. Nowell muses. "Maybe tonight you can be the crow."

"Whad'da you mean?"

"C-CAPS. We're like crows after the power company."

Danny smiles inside himself. *Mr. Nowell thinks like me. We shoud'a called ourselves Crows.*

"Think about it," Mr. Nowell says. "We're against the pumped storage. We think it will change our river, wash out nesting areas and kill lots of fish. Jeff would lose his business if fishermen stop fishing Pepin. The Cookie Lady is afraid the fish kill will stink up

Lake Pepin and tourists won't come to buy her apples. The Boat Lady would move to another marina with other boaters. Then, there's the people who'd come to the Water Skiing Festival. All down sides."

"What do you mean, down sides?" Danny asks.

"A down side is something that isn't good—or something you don't want. But if there's a down side then there's probably an up side for someone else."

Danny takes off his cap, and rubs his forehead. He traces the Twins' emblem while he listens.

"With the pump storage, the power company will grow bigger and stronger and make more profit. People who have invested in the company will earn dividends, and they'll get richer. People who work for the power company will have jobs. And, then, there are the people who use the electricity. It will keep their lights on and their computers running. They'll be able to do their jobs and make money too."

"Sounds complicated."

"It is. Probably too complicated for crows, but not for us." He grunts with a chuckle. When they reach Lake City, Mr. Nowell turns off Highway 61 and parks in front of Jeff's store behind a van painted in camouflage colors. Through the front store window, Danny sees the Norwegian settled on a chair.

What's he doin' here? Danny hesitates and waits in the truck until Mr. Nowell motions him to come. He shuffles through the shop door. The Norwegian looks at him with a spark of recognition. Danny shudders and looks at the floor.

Jeff greets Mr. Nowell with a hand shake and slaps Danny on the back. He invites everyone to pour a cup of coffee and eat Snickerdoodle cookies made by the Cookie Lady. Four new people have joined C-CAPS, including the Norwegian, who says he's a nature guy. *Doesn't say he lives in a tent in Snake Creek Valley.*

Jeff calls the meeting to order and reviews the proposed Pump Storage project, reading a description from a printed brochure:

A 185 acre upper reservoir built like a ring dike
Five miles south of Lake City above Lake Pepin
An underground power station with tunnels and shafts
All together a 2,100 foot conductor system

The Cookie Lady shrieks, "That's my backyard." She teeters on her chair and spills her coffee. Jeff hands her a roll of paper towels, and he continues reading.

"Pepin water would be pumped 1200 feet up the bluff then released to go 900 feet down the bluff."

Mrs. Honeydo pokes her husband. "Honey, are the river bluffs really that high?"

Mr. Honeydo shakes his head.

"Sounds like the makings of a great water park," adds Mr. Nowell. "But not for the fish."

Jeff goes on. "There would be pumping units, a switch yard, new roads and tunnels. Yes, and probably dead fish, though it doesn't say so in the brochure."

"PU." Mrs. Honeydo holds her nose, shakes her head and sticks out her tongue at Danny. He chokes on a bite of cookie and laughs.

The Boat Lady stands up and clears her throat. She wears a dark sailor suit trimmed with white anchors and a matching hat that sits on the back of her silver-gray hair. She reminds the group she owns a sailboat in the marina and has navigated the Mississippi from St. Anthony Falls to St. Louis. "Here's what we need to do." She waves a sheaf of papers at the group. "I didn't make enough copies, you'll have to share." Danny gets a copy and sits closer to Mr. Nowell. The man smells like aftershave. *When I start shavin,' I'll buy his brand.*

Danny closes his eyes. He imagines everyone in the circle having black-feathered wings instead of arms and yellow claws instead of feet. *We're the advanced guard. The Boat Lady is the Head Crow.*

"This is our strategy," the Boat Lady says, who has now

become the head Crow. "Let's review the process, make a time line, list the agencies involved, decide what steps to take and what people to talk to."

"Aha!" Jeff and Mr. Nowell say together.

"I'm a good organizer," she crows with a note of glee in her voice, and a tickle of a giggle.

"Good work," Mr. Honeydo says with a nod. He bounces his bushy white hair.

Mrs. Crow continues. "Their process began two years ago. Government agencies raised concerns about water quality, fishing, lock and dam operations, release of water downriver and falling rocks on the bluff." Danny listens to new words he's never heard before: entrainment, limnology, turbulence, turbidity, sedimentation, erosion, bluff stability, and overwinter fish stress. *Makes my head spin. How'd a woman get so smart?*

He puts his feet on the rung of the chair and rests his elbows on his knees. He looks at the floor of wide boards and notices the Norwegian's boots, heavy boots with thick soles. Boots made for walking up bluff sidings and through underbrush.

Mrs. Crow shuffles her papers. "This is the time line. We have sixty days to protest and two weeks have already gone by."

The group inhales in one breath, except for Mr. Nowell, who grunts.

"We better get busy," says the Cookie Lady. She scratches the top of her head.

Mrs. Crow lists the agencies that have been involved in previous meetings: Public Service, Public Utilities Commission, Dept. of Natural Resources, Pollution Control, Environmental Quality Board, Federal Energy Regulatory Commission, the power company and the Minnesota Attorney General. She ends by listing the names of people and groups C-CAPS needs to contact. "We need callers and letter writers. Who will volunteer?"

Everyone, except the Norwegian, raises a hand. Mrs. Crow gives Danny two names. Mr. Nowell takes a page. He leans close and whispers, "We'll have a 'write-a-thon' tomorrow."

"Better than goin' trout fishin'," Danny whispers back. "I ain't fishin' with Walter and his water worms ever again."

When the meeting is over, Danny sidles up to the Snickerdoodles and takes two. The Norwegian moves close and does the same. He looks at Danny.

"Ain't I seen you fishin' at Snake Creek?"

A Name

"WORDS ARE POWERFUL," Mr. Nowell says. "Here's a way to get your letter organized." He and Danny sit at the kitchen table Saturday morning. The man lists four words on the page: Hey-You-Say-So. "Your first sentence is the '*catcher*.' The second is a '*you*' hook. Then, you describe the problem, and finally, you tell the reader what to do."

Danny thinks hard and writes under Hey: Do dead fish stink? He holds his nose and grunts like Mr. Nowell. Under You he writes: Have you ever gone fishing on Lake Pepin? He continues writing: A pumped storage project is being proposed. The power company will pump water from Lake Pepin into a reservoir on top of a bluff by Lake City and then release the water to make electricity. The level of Lake Pepin will go up and down every day.

"How do I spell fluctuating?" he asks.

Mr. Nowell laughs and spells out the word. "Say something about the narrows of the river downstream, how the fluctuating water will wash away bird nests, beaver lodges, and muskrat houses. Tell how pumping the water into the reservoir and then releasing it into Lake Pepin will kill fish."

"How do I spell reservoir?" Danny listens, writes, then puts down his pencil. "When me and Anne went on her turtle mission, before we found the dead lady, she told me people stopped a power plant by McCarthy Lake. They saved the Blandings."

"Now, it's more than turtles, it's a whole lake and river," Mr. Nowell says. He helps Danny write the last paragraph: So, Minnesota's government agencies have tried to stop the pumped storage, but it's a federal project and only you as a voter and a citizen can do the job. We have six weeks to make a difference. Please write a letter to the power company and tell them to stop.

Mr. Nowell nods. Danny copies his letter without the Hey, You, Say and So and signs it Danny Malloy. He holds the letter up and admires his words at arms length. Danny reads the letter aloud:

Dear Mississippi River Lover,

Do you think dead fish stink?

Have you ever gone fishing on Lake Pepin?

A pumped storage project is being proposed. The power company will pump water from Lake Pepin into a reservoir on top of a bluff by Lake City and then release the water to make electricity. The level of Lake Pepin will go up and down every day. The pumping will kill fish. The fluctuating water will wash away bird nests, beaver lodges, and muskrat houses down river.

Minnesota's government agencies have tried to stop the pumped storage, but it's a federal project and only you as a voter and a citizen can do the job. We have six weeks to make a difference. Please write a letter to the power company and tell them to stop.

Sincerely,

Danny Malloy

"It's only missing Samurai. Danny Malloy, Samurai."

Call me by my name
Danny Malloy, Samurai
Hear my battle cry

Danny jumps on his chair and shouts "Ahee!" like a Ninja in the movies. He poses, one arm above his head, the other thrust out holding an imaginary saber.

Mr. Nowell pushes away his chair and matches Danny's stance. He stomps his foot on the floor and stabs at Danny's middle with a powerful push. Danny responds with a laugh. He jumps off the chair and they duel around the kitchen table until Mrs. Nowell calls, "Time." She steps between them like a referee.

Mr. Nowell grunts and folds both Mrs. Nowell and Danny into a great bear hug.

"Call this a Samurai squish," he says. He releases them with a grunt, and wipes his forehead with his shirt sleeve.

On Tuesday, Danny bikes to town, and buys three copies of the local weekly. He cuts out his letters and sends one to Jenny and one to his mother. The third copy he puts under his mattress with the girly magazines. *Someday, I'll show this to my dad.*

WEST NEWTON

DANNY SITS WITH the Nowells on their deck after a breakfast of blueberry pancakes. He wears a shirt with a Twins patch, and holds a warm cup of coffee against his belly.

A golden ball of sun melts the morning into white light. High winds sweep streaks of contrails across the sky. A lacy moon hangs in the western sky reluctant to disappear. Down on the river bank, two resident herons squawk over territory.

"If they're going to change the river," Mr. Nowell says, stretching out his legs and hooking his toes on the bottom deck board, "I'm going to visit West Newton." Mrs. Nowell matches his stretch and taps his toe with hers. Neither Nowell wears shoes.

"You just want an excuse to go fishing," she chides.

He pulls back his long legs and tugs his shirt around his chest. He wiggles his toes on top of hers. "I think I'll show Danny my old glory hole."

"What's a glory hole?" Danny asks.

"A secret place," Mr. Nowell says in a stage whisper, "with lots of fish."

"Trout?"

"No trout, just catfish, northerns, sunnies, crappies and silvers. West Newton was my buddy hangout."

"West Newton? Where's West Newton?"

"East of McCarthy Lake, across the way from the Weaver

Dunes, a nice place. We can fish or nap. Maybe Sue will come with us, or bring us lunch?" He grabs her hand. "What do you think?"

"Lunch," Mrs. Nowell agrees with a nod.

When Mr. Nowell and Danny finish their barn chores, they load fishing tackle, sodas and a sack of potato chips into the truck. At Kellogg, Mr. Nowell stops at Curly's Bait Shop to buy willowcats. The sale takes a long time, while the men swap fishing stories. Mr. Nowell ends up buying ten lures to catch northerns and a paper cup of *cats*. Danny's glad to see there's no water worms.

Back in the truck, Mr. Nowell steers southward toward the tall smoke stacks at Alma, across the river. They pass a row of grand houses with trimmed lawns and gardens. The blacktop road dissolves into gravel, and they enter a world of oak and pine. Mr. Nowell slows the truck to a stop. Ahead, a turquoise bird splashes in a mud puddle.

"Indigo Bunting," Mr. Nowell says. "Beautiful bird, very special."

Mr. Nowell leans against the steering wheel. "What color would you say he is?"

"Blue. Brighter than any bird I've ever seen."

"I call him iridescent turquoise. The one thing that makes him so special is that his feathers are really black. Only the way he reflects light makes him look that brilliant blue. His wife is very drab, a brown color."

"Oh," Danny says.

"And he's a night flier," Mr. Nowell continues, "migrates thousands of miles and uses the stars to guide him."

"How do you know all that?"

"I've talked to him," the man says and chuckles. "Remember the Indigo Bunting, he brings good luck."

When the bird finishes bathing, it flutters away in a bright streak. Mr. Nowell shifts the truck to low and drives into a parking lot filled with cars and trailers. "Too bad for the early birds," he says, getting out of the truck, "they missed the Indigo. Our reward for being late."

A channel of the Mississippi rushes between the parking lot and dense bushes and trees that hide the houses of West Newton, though a few chimneys peek above the tree tops. At the north end of the parking lot, a road crosses a gated bridge.

"Beyond those gates," Mr. Nowell says, "fishing shacks grew to become mighty fine houses with the help of carpenters. Most are owned by people from Rochester."

"Can we cross the bridge?" Danny asks.

"We'd be trespassing."

"Oh!" Danny stiffens. *Trespassing. Don't want to end up in jail.*

Mr. Nowell notes Danny's body language. "I guess, when I was a kid, things were different. We didn't worry about trespassing, we just did."

"Like how?"

"When I was your age, I lived in Rochester. My gang came down to West Newton most every weekend. Forty miles. My friend, Mike, had a car. We'd all chip in to fill the gas tank, twenty-five cents. There were usually six of us. We'd come down on a Friday night, stay the weekend, skinny dip, and jug."

"Huh?" Danny smiles and thinks about his magic hooch. He lifts an imaginary bottle to his lips.

"No, no!" Mr. Nowell laughs. "That's a different kind of jugging. We did drink a beer or two, but jugging was fishing. We'd tie a fishing line to a bleach bottle, bait the hook with a silver and toss the whole works in the river."

"Silver? Money? You paid the fish to catch 'em?"

Mr. Nowell laughs.

"No, fish, little silver fish, minnows," he says. "Catfish loved them. Then, we'd take the cats to Pepin, to the big fish market. There, they paid good money—" Mr. Nowell tweaks his fingers. "It's not there, anymore. The people at Pepin cleaned the fish, and shipped them off to Chicago, St. Louis or New Orleans."

"So, what did you do with the money?"

"Bought more gas, maybe beer, or hot dogs."

Danny mimics drinking from a jug. Mr. Nowell punches his shoulder with a quick jab.

"So, this was your glory hole and all you did was fish?"

Mr. Nowell unbuttons the top of his shirt, as if basking in his memories makes him warm. "When we weren't fishing, we'd skinny-dip or lie out in the sun and bake off our butts. Today we'd have trouble with a VanOort, but then, only our mothers complained. They could tell by our sunburns."

"And girls?" Danny asks, feeling brave. "Skinny-dipping and all?"

"Sometimes girls from around here visited, but it was mostly us guys. One guy brought girly magazines, but he never shared. Two guys who worked the canning factory in Plainview joined us, but when they got here, all they did was sleep."

"Sounds like Hamm," Danny muses as he stretches. "Did you gamble, play Farkle?"

"No, can't say we did."

Mr. Nowell motions Danny to follow him on a path along the river to a wall of limestone rocks. A metal plate reads *WPA, 1934.*

"WPA, Works Programs Administration, " Mr. Nowell explains, "paid men to work, when they couldn't find jobs. The government hired guys to make this a park. Flood waters have washed away some of this landing." He sits on a smooth rock ledge, motioning Danny beside him. "Now we don't have to worry about everything washing away, we can watch everything die."

"You mean the pumped storage?"

Mr. Nowell nods. "Everything's changing."

They watch the river flow down the channel for a few minutes, then, leave the landing, walk back to the truck, retrieve their fishing gear and settle on a grassy spot. Danny baits a willowcat on his hook, casts out and remembers Walter's coaching. *Let the northern move the willowcat in its mouth before reeling in.* He catches a fish, big enough for frying, though it puts up a fight.

"Nice job," Mr. Nowell praises, helping Danny net the fish. "Three pounds, at least."

Mr. Nowell catches two saugers and a spike-toothed pike. The pike is slippery, with a long nose and a mouth full of sharp teeth. The saugers look like northerns. He releases the pike and puts the other fish on a stringer. "We'll have fish for supper," the man says.

I'm glad we fish for food, Danny moogles, remembering Walter's words.

At noon, Mrs. Nowell delivers a picnic basket of fried chicken and brownies. Danny helps her spread out a blanket. She's brought chicken with crispy skin, and the brownies are gooey, with an inch of fudge frosting. He takes a brownie.

Eat dessert first
Suck fingers, then, crunch chicken
Save the rest for last

THE REAL GLORY HOLE

AFTER LUNCH AND a short nap, Mr. Nowell motions Danny to follow. "Come, I want to show you another part of my old Glory Hole." North of the parking lot, they wade through tall grasses to a grove of oaks, cedars, birch and sumac. "This is where we took the new guys." Mr. Nowell points to a couple of tree stumps close together. "Our initiation spot." He plants his feet and puts his hands on his hips. "Now, in river talk, a glory hole is a place where you always catch fish. Good fishermen know their glory holes and keep them secret. Here, at this glory hole, our fish were suckers of a different sort."

"Like stonerollers or redhorses?"

"You're good, Danny boy, but no." The man puts his arm on Danny's shoulder. "Over there was an old chicken coop." He points to a clearing between two burr oaks. "Gone now, but you know the kind? Looks like a chunk of tunnel. It was a kind of office with insulation, maybe put up for the WPA. The mice loved it. And right beside it was this cow pasture with Jerseys, brown cows, the kind with big eyes."

"So, we'd come to Newton and do our jugging. Before they built the parking lot, everything was wide open." He stretches his hand toward the stumps. "The gang never slept in the chicken coop because of the mice, but we'd invite the new guys, as a sort of welcome, to take advantage of our deluxe accommodations."

Mr. Nowell says deluxe accommodations with a grin and raises his eyebrows.

"One night there's this guy, Jack, a doctor's kid, from Rochester. Smart and cocky. He drives a new car, but won't let us ride with him, and he brings a fancy sleeping bag. So he settles down in our accommodations. We're all waiting, sitting around the fire. There's this bomber's moon. Remember, what I called a bomber's moon? Bright as daylight. Then, we hear Jack scream. The mice have crawled into his sleeping bag. He comes barreling through the door just as the Jerseys are tromping to the river. He runs plumb into the side of one big cow. She panics, moos to the moon, and gushers out a vile, green stream. We could all smell it. Jack slips in it and falls. Then, he yells even louder, and the cows stampede off in all directions. We run for our lives and hide behind the trees." Mr. Nowell laughs, bends and slaps his knees.

"Jack's wearing pajamas, silk for all I know, and they're all wet and shitty. He peels them off and heads for the river just a screaming. By then, there are cows in the river, wading and splashing around, mooing and grunting, still agitated. So, Jack ends up swimming naked with a bunch of cows." Mr. Nowell wipes his eyes. "Jack never came back." The man takes a deep breath. "Fun to remember and sad to think they'll be changing our river. If we let them," he says, as an afterthought.

C-CAPS Attacks

DANNY THINKS ABOUT glory holes as he rides with Mr. Nowell to Lake City and the next C-CAPS meeting.

Guess I've got glory holes. Those nights at the park back home, when me and the guys planned hold-ups, drank hooch and smoked Marlboros. We bucked the new kids off the horse and called them asses. Not like mice and cow shit. At Hamm, we didn't plan hold-ups, since some guys had already done that, but we played Farkle. New guys got cheated and there was lots of girl talk. Mostly braggin'.

If I went back to Hamm, I'd tell about the riverboat. How I snuck aboard the River Princess, helping Walter unload garbage. I'd brag about Elizabeth, the most beautiful girl, ever. When I close my eyes, I can still smell her honeysuckle perfume. Goosebumps crawl up Danny's arms.

Elizabeth snuck me on board. Shook her boobs by the ship's checker and got him all excited. We rolled dice for kisses. I think Elizabeth wanted to lose. Danny quivers as he remembers the tingles he felt. *When we reached St. Paul, I met Elizabeth's GrandPeppy. He was something else, like a crow with a spiffy gold cane and shiny, black shoes. He took us swing-dancing in the Wabasha Caves. Told stories about gangsters and ghosts and showed us real bullet holes in the cave's wall. He drank his liquor straight, not beer, like the guys at Joe's.*

If I went back to Hamm, I wouldn't tell how it ended, how the riverboat checker wouldn't let me back on the boat 'cause I weren't on his list and Elizabeth couldn't do no shaken' with her GrandPeppy there. Then the old man paid the checker a hundred dollars to get rid of me, but the checker had heart, let me ride the riverboat back to Alma. The Nowells called my ride an adventure, and didn't report me to Jenny.

Danny shifts on the truck seat and looks across the river. His Elizabeth adventure had happened in the spring, before his vacation died, before the dead woman and before VanOort knew he was JD. *Gotta stay clean or I'll be back at Hamm, telling my story. VanOort don't like foster kids.*

Mr. Nowell eases the truck into a parking space in front of Jeff's store. Danny walks through the door and sees the Norwegian. He shivers and shoves away his guilty feelings. *Geeze! Just 'cause he lives in a tent does he think he owns Snake Creek Valley?*

"Our letters and phone calls are working," Jeff says, talking over the buzz of people. "More people have joined the C-CAPS fight. An attorney in St. Paul wants to donate his services." Everyone claps. A new guy from Rochester, who wears a white shirt, blue suit and red tie, says he has the names of important people, politically. George, another new guy, has contacted important friends in Washington D.C. Jeff holds up a letter.

"The Isaac Walton League pledges to help. Even the Minnesota government guys have scheduled workshops to tell people the bad news, like the bluffs are porous and we could have a car wash on Highway 61." The group hollers and claps, stomping their feet. The walls shake. Danny looks up. The tin-ceiling tiles quiver. The Cookie Lady wipes her eyes and the Honeydos clap their hands together in a high five. Jeff collects more hundred dollar bills, and even the Norwegian takes out his wallet.

"We're swinging in the tree tops," Mr. Nowell whispers to Danny. "We just need to keep the racket up and wait for the power company to break cover." He grunts and pats Danny's knee. "How does it feel to be an old crow?"

BACK TO SNAKE CREEK

"SORRY BOY." DANNY gives Yago an extra scoop of oats. "It's a bicycle day. I need time to figure stuff out." The horse gives him a sad, brown-eyed look and nuzzles his nose in the oats. "Goin' to visit Sky Star, then headin' down to Snake Creek. Jenny says, Samurai pay attention to the small stuff, and I got this feelin' the dead lady, the coyote, the Indian and the Norwegian are all connected. But I gotta do my thinkin' alone. Walter's too know-it-all and Anne's too bossy. Even you'd be a bother."

Danny cleans the barn stalls, puts the horses out to pasture, then heads for breakfast. A gray morning mist covers the Nowells' yard and stretches across the river. The sun shines through the foggy air like a silver quarter.

He changes from his barn clothes to shorts and a tee. and spends ten minutes combing his hair, looking for a way to look older. Soon school starts and he's not a football hero, like Walter. He borrows Mr. Nowell's hair gel.

The fog makes biking slow on Highway 61. Cars appear out of nowhere, some with their lights on, some coming at him like gray ghosts. The bike's tires throw up wet gravel behind him, making a 'thump-e-d-thump' noise. He stops at Sky Star's grave. White egg shells are spewed about, evidence of turtles that will never be. He's glad Mrs. Nowell's bushel baskets protected their turtle nursery until the rains came.

Danny kicks between some bushes hoping he has overlooked the spade. Or, it has decided to reveal itself, having a life of its own. Nothing. A sharp buckthorn scratches his legs. *Wish I'd worn long pants.* He finds two candy wrappers, Nut Goodies, and shoves them in his pocket.

Back on 61, he bikes to Snake Creek Valley road, slowing down where he and Walter got the water worms. He rubs his nose. He remembers how the worms made his hands stink. *If I ever go trout fishing again, I'll get bait at Curly's.*

Danny heads up the Snake Creek Road, past the goat prairie and the Norwegian's campsite. At a turn-around spot where the gravel road widens, he brakes and pulls his bike into the tall grass. The steep road grade makes his heart pound. He crouches, resting his elbows on his knees, his eyes level with the moving grass heads. He pretends he's a Samurai scout watching, waiting, and listening.

> *Sing me your secret*
> *Let the Snake Creek green ladies*
> *Dance me their magic*

Slowly, the sun burns away the fog curtain, sending wispy puffs of gray rolling up the steep bluffs. Danny rubs his calves. Behind his knees, sweat trickles down to his ankles. He's a Samurai ready to spring into action. Time seems to stand still. A doe and her two fawns amble down the road in front of him. *Wish I had a gun.* He takes aim and pretends to kill her. *That makes the young ones foster kids. I guess, I'd rather have a watch.* He looks at his bare wrist.

Footsteps approach, then a wet nose pokes his ear and a wet tongue slurps across his cheek and knocks him on his butt, his legs spread out in front of him. The coyote-dog grins an almost human smile. The Norwegian stands on the roadside. He carries a gun, a rifle or shotgun. Danny's too scared to tell. His heart beats in triple time.

"Well, if it ain't Danny boy." The Norwegian grabs Danny's wrists and pulls him to his feet. "Whatcha doin' here?"

Danny plants his feet for balance then steps back. "Just thinkin', I guess."

"Saw you and your friend, the Indian kid, fishin.' Catch anything?"

"Trout. Fried up real good. Used water worms. It's the Indian way," Danny says. "But, I'd rather buy bait." He uses his 'be charming' chatter, a defense he has with cops, PO's, and foster moms. *What does this guy want, and why's he got a gun?*

"Did you see the Indian?" The Norwegian shifts his gun from shoulder to shoulder.

Danny frowns. "Indian? You mean Walter?"

"No, the old guy. I see him sometimes when I'm fishin'."

"You mean he's real?"

"About as real, as a ghost can be. Sometimes he comes by camp. Then, he's just a spot of light floating by. Makes the dog whimper."

"Really?"

The Norwegian nods. "Been here a long time, since Snake Creek Valley belonged to the Indians." He swallows. His Adam's apple moves up and down. "Nowell your real dad?"

"Naw. My foster dad."

"Wondered, seems pretty up-tight. You know what I mean? Anxious about that pump thing."

"Ain't we all?"

"Guess some people call it progress." The dog moves beside the Norwegian and sits with its ears alert.

"Your dog?" Danny asks.

"Adopted me. Came around camp beggin' for food."

"Is it a real dog? Saw it fishin'. Thought it was a coyote."

"Probably is…anyway part of him…maybe. He's friendly and we talk. Gets lonesome at night with just owls, crickets, frogs and ghosts." The man laughs at his words.

"Know what you mean," Danny says. "I got real lonesome

here at first. Definitely ain't no action. No people." He kicks at the gravel road. "Like you say, owls, crickets, and frogs. Can't say ghosts, 'cause I only saw him once."

The Norwegian shifts his gun on his shoulder.

"So whatcha huntin'?" Danny smiles like he does for the judge.

"Something for supper. Rabbit. Squirrel. Ever eat squirrel?"

"Nope."

"Tastes like chicken. Redder. Chewier. The dog and I both like it. I get the breast, he gets the rest." The Norwegian swings his gun off his shoulder and pulls a Nut Goodie from inside his vest. He peels off the wrapper, drops it on the road, breaks off a chunk of chocolate and offers it to Danny.

"Gotta get goin'. Nice talkin'. When you get home better take a shower with something strong, a brown soap like FelsNaptha. You're sittin' in a pile of poison ivy." He points to shiny green leaves and chuckles, swallowing the words he says to himself. He crosses the road, then heads down the steep bank to Snake Creek. Coyote-dog follows. Danny listens until the man's footsteps fade away.

Danny picks up the Nut Goodie wrapper and shoves it in his pocket with the others from Sky Star's grave. *Three mysteries solved. There's an Indian ghost, the dog's a coyote with a human face and the Norwegian eats Nut Goodies. Two mysteries left. Where's Walter's knapsack and where was the Norwegian when Anne and me found the dead lady?*

GW Calls

"Hey Li'l Bro, how you doin'?" Danny hears GW's voice boom across the wire. GW doesn't wait for an answer. "Callin' to tell ya we're comin'. Need a place ta meet ya. Don't want to butt in at that foster place. Need a place close by, private like, where Bobbie and I can drink a beer or two."

"Geeze! I don't know." Danny laughs. "Given up drinkin' these days."

"No hooch?" GW teases back. Danny imagines his brother's grin.

"Right. No Joe's. Even given up smokin." The sound of his brother's voice warms him like a big hug.

"Cripes. Your life is really dead. One of these damn days you'll be knockin' on the pearly gates singin' hymns with Grandma." He hums a bit of their grandma's favorite song, somethin' about meetin' at the river. "Look around for a meetin' place for us, but don't say nothin, specially to those foster folks. They won't understand, and sure as hell don't tell that Hamm witch."

"Huh?" *Jenny?*

"Take care Li'l Bro. I'll call ya again, tomorrow maybe."

Danny hears the phone click and the dial tone buzz.

"My brother." Danny says and hangs up the phone. The Nowells sit at their kitchen table drinking coffee.

"What did he say?" Mrs. Nowell rolls her cup between her

hands, shrugging her shoulders like she's cold, how she does her thinking. "Is he planning a trip to Deadwood?" She smiles, but Danny knows it's not for real.

"Think so. Not Deadwood but Sturgis with the hog guys."

"Has he talked to Jenny?"

Danny shrugs his shoulders. "Don't know."

"Well, they went last summer," Mr. Nowell pats his wife's hand and adds under his breath, "and came back. Shouldn't be a problem."

"Did you ride the motorcycle?" She moves her cup between her hands and spills coffee.

Mr. Nowell grabs a napkin.

"A hog." Danny clenches his fists like he's holding the cycles' handle bars. He feels the motor's pulse between his thighs. He hears the roar of the motors. He remembers the evening campfires, smoking sticks, hog talk, drinking beer and sex talk.

"What did you see?" Mrs. Nowell asks.

"Lots of road." He smiles his charming way. "South Dakota and all those presidents carved on the side of a mountain. And a big Indian ridin' a horse," he adds.

"Crazy Horse," Mr. Nowell says. "Impressive."

"Who went with, besides your brother?" Mrs. Nowell rolls her cup again.

"A bunch of guys. Never used names, just handles: Lonesome, Speedy, Slick, John-John, and Alligator. They called me Hooch." He doesn't tell the Nowells why they called him Hooch, but GW had told the guys about the Joe's collection bottle.

The Nowells exchange glances.

"Good guys?" she asks.

"Just let it be for now, Sue," Mr. Nowell says.

"I know, but I worry." She frowns and rolls her cup between her hands until she spills her coffee again.

> *GW had it right*
> *Don't tell 'em he's a comin'*
> *Best kept a secret*

MEETIN' AT THE RIVER

DANNY LIKES SITTING with Mr. Nowell on a Sunday afternoon
drinking Dr. Pepper and eating popcorn. The Twins beat the
Brewers. Baseball allegiance along the river is equally divided
between Minnesota and Wisconsin. Danny favors the Twins who
win this time. Mr. Nowell pays his buck and threatens, "There'll
be a next time."

Danny isn't into sports like Walter, who will be the quarterback
at high school this fall. Today's baseball game is early with daylight
left and time to ride. Danny cinches Yago's saddle, steps into the
stirrups and swings onto the palomino's back.

Need time for thinkin'
My big bro don't like Jenny
Wants a secret place

Yago steps out, eager to go. A week has gone by since he has
been ridden and given an extra scoop of oats.

Danny guides the horse along a familiar path following
the river. All spring they rode after school. Danny watched the
Mississippi flyway come alive with honking geese and noisy tundra
swans headed north. He watched a pair of wood ducks teach
their young to swim, and marveled how both the parents took

responsibility. He'd thought about his own folks, and wondered, *what made my dad go away?*

Piles of white clouds in the blue sky make him think of afternoons with his grandmother, rocking with her on her front porch. She sang to him. She liked hymns. He remembers one about the river: "We shall gather at the river, the river, the river. We shall gather at the river—" He can't remember all the words except it ends with '*the throne of God*'. He looks up. His grandmother said, '*God sits on those white clouds*'.

Across the river, the Samurai dragon guards the green bluffs. The boaters have called it a day. Night creatures have yet to begin their mating songs. Down stream a white tow pushes its barges toward Lock and Dam #4 at Alma. Danny talks to Yago.

"Why'd GW call Jenny a witch?" The words sting. "I love Jenny."

Yago stops and bends his head to munch grass. Danny gives him a nudge with his knee. "What do you think is goin' on?" he asks the horse. "Does GW have a plan? Somethin' he doesn't want Jenny to know, somethin' about South Dakota?" He shrugs his shoulders. "I think the best place to meet is at Snake Creek." He tugs the reins, turns Yago towards Nowells and sings: "We shall gather at the river, the river, the river. We shall gather at the Snake and plan a trip to Sturgis."

A Secret Place

DANNY IS KILLING time, paging through Mr. Nowell's magazine and looking at pictures of the Mississippi River. He jumps when the phone rings. Mrs. Nowell answers. "Danny, your brother." She sounds snippy.

Danny picks up the phone and hunches his shoulders towards the wall, cupping his hand over his lips and the receiver. He tells GW about the Snake Creek Valley Road and where to turn off Highway 61. He'll wait for him next Sunday at a picnic spot, close to the highway, before the Bend in the River, where he met the Norwegian and the coyote-dog.

"Okay. Next Sunday, but be careful, Li'l Bro." GW warns. "There'll be lots of hogs on the road revving up for the Flood Run this fall. Riders come from all over Minnesota. It's an annual thing, somethin' the hogs did back in '65 to clean up after a flood."

"I'll be careful," Danny promises. "I'll stay on the old road and take the plank bridge 'cross the Zumbro."

"Good. About two o'clock. And Danny," he says, as if it's an afterthought, "bring the eagle jacket."

"The eagle jacket?" Danny scratches the top of his head.

"Ya, my jacket, the blue-velvet with the eagle on the back? You got it?"

"Sure, I'll bring it." Danny gulps. The jacket still hangs in

Mrs. Nowell's closet. She's kept it since he rented the silver-toed boots, not even giving it back when he went home to help his mom move.

"Good. See you Li'l Bro."

He hangs up the phone and sees Mrs. Nowell leaning her back against the kitchen counter, listening.

"My bro."

She nods, waiting for more words. Her stare makes his heart thump, like she already knows about the eagle jacket. He can't talk, he doesn't dare. He might say the wrong words. He heads for the bathroom and locks the door.

Meet Snake Creek at two
Listen for the hogs and bring
The eagle jacket

Snake Creek Wish

The next Sunday, hogs swarm like angry bees. Danny brakes his bike on the shoulder of Highway 61 and watches the riders zoom by, dressed in black leathers, some with helmets, most wearing goggles. Their radios buzz louder than the sound of their engines.

The hogs go on forever. No break in the traffic. He wheels off the shoulder and goes back over the railroad to CR 30, the old 61. CR 30 needs repair, more than repair. The bridge over the Zumbro has been replaced with wide planks. He wheels his bike across, pedals through Kellogg, past Curly's Bait Shop, and heads south.

Old CR 30 connects with Highway 61 just north of Snake Creek Valley Road. The hogs sound like thunder. He waits for a break in the traffic, finally reaches Snake Valley Creek Road, and bikes past the goat pasture bluff, huffing as the road ascends. Today he's not grinning and spinning.

He turns into the Norwegian's tent site, curious to see the coyote-dog. The tent is gone, the wood pile, gone, the chair and table, gone. The Norwegian has moved.

Danny swings his bike around and heads toward the picnic site, his waiting place for GW. The parking lot is empty. No picnickers, no bikers nor campers. He climbs on a wooden table, sits and waits. He looks at his wrist. His thoughts pile up like big white clouds. *Wish I had a watch. Wish I had a pocket knife. Wish I could bring my dad back.* He's wrapped the eagle jacket in a plastic bag and tied it to the back of his bike.

The afternoon sun moves slowly. He stretches, gets up and bikes around the clearing a couple of times, spinning sand. He heads down a path, following a sign to the creek that warns *'Watch for Rattlesnakes'*. At the creek, he looks into the clear water. No trout, but a redhorse ambles along the bottom over a floor of golden oak leaves. He shrugs off a familiar feeling of being watched, shifts his shoulders, and scans the brush for the coyote-dog or the Indian ghost. Nothing. He bikes to a point that overlooks Rattlesnake Ridge and then hurries back to the picnic area.

Danny sits back on the picnic table, resting his elbows on his knees. He puts his chin in the palms of his hands. *Wish there were some people here. Like Bobbie. She makes me feel grown-up. When I get old, I'll have a hog and a girl like her. A real girl friend.* He closes his eyes, lies back on the table, and practices kissing his forearm. *I've never really had a girl, one that kissed and did stuff. The guys at Hamm talked girls and sex. The guys at Joe's talked sex, too. Sometimes they were married, sometimes not. Wonder if the Nowells ever do it?* He sits up and sees three turkeys strut through the picnic space. They stretch their long legs and gobble-gobble, ignoring him.

"Bang, Bang," he shoots an imaginary rifle. "Gotcha!" The turkeys waddle off.

Elizabeth could have been a girlfriend. He closes his eyes and sniffs. *Honeysuckle. Then there was Maggie, another girl dancing at the Wabasha Caves, wearing cowboy boots and telling me to go back to the Nowells. She was a foster kid, too. Why is it, everyone wants to tell me what I should do?*

He leans his elbows on his knees and presses his fingers to his forehead. He sees Anne hardened under her wet, red shirt. *Shit, I don't want Anne for a girlfriend. She's bossy, besides she ratted on me, got me in bad with VanOort.* The thought of Anne makes him antsy. Suddenly, he's in a swarm of bugs, black gnats. He waves his hands then scratches his head, his arms, between his legs, all over. His thoughts rush over him. *Bugs! I need Walter's halo. I need a knife. I wish I had a watch. What's happened to GW and Bobbie?*

The cloud of gnats move on. Danny stretches out again on the picnic table, lying on his back, kicking his heels against the boards. The sky goes up forever. He replays in his mind how the coyote's nose became the Norwegian's face and then the Norwegian's face became the old Indian's face. *Is Snake Creek haunted, stalked by an old Dakota who refused to move on?* He thinks about the half-breed tract, Reads Landing washed away, and the Blanding turtles. Now, the power company threatens the whole river. *Why did the Norwegian leave his camp after paying a hundred dollars to C-CAPS? Where'd he go?*

The sun slips behind a western bluff and a silent shadow falls across the picnic area. He threads his arms through the sleeves of the eagle jacket, smoothing his cheek against the blue-velvet. His stomach growls reminding him it's suppertime. In the distance, the hogs still roar. *It's late.* He imagines GW skidding down the highway in a tumble, riding the tarvy on a shoulder or a knee. *Hope he wore his helmet. And Bobbie? She'll make going to Sturgis really fun.*

Danny leaves Snake Creek. At the Nowell's barn door, he takes off the jacket and stuffs it in the plastic bag. He slides into the barn, shimmies to the loft and hides the bag under a bale of hay.

The smell of pizza welcomes him into the Nowell's kitchen.

"You're late," Mr. Nowell says.

"Sorry," Danny answers, "been to Snake Creek."

"See any trout?"

"Nope, just a redhorse and some turkeys."

"There's pizza on the cupboard," Mrs. Nowell says.

Wish I could ask, has GW called.

> *Hey, I've been waitin'*
> *Don't want to spill your secret*
> *GW, ring up fast*

Change Of Plans

"We got a problem Li'l Bro," GW says. Bobbie's hog crashed. Bad. That's why I'm callin'." Danny holds the phone tight to his ear and faces the wall. His hair is still wet from a shower, after weeding for hours in Mrs. Nowells' flowers.

"Is Bobbie hurt?"

"Naw, she ain't hurt. It's her hog. Now we got only one hog for Sturgis. It's either her or you, kid, and you know you ain't no fun to sleep with."

"I can't go?" Danny shakes his head, disbelieving. Sirens scream in his head.

"We'll do it next year."

GW's words echo far off. Danny's insides twist.

"Can't you fix her?" He protests. *There's got to be a way. Why does everything bad happen to me?*

"Sure I can fix 'er, but then there ain't no money left for Sturgis. It's a hard place, Danny, hate to disappoint ya, but I got this feelin'. If Bobbie don't get to Sturgis with me, she'll go with someone else."

Danny thumps the wall. "Hey Bro! I got money from the boots."

"That's nice of you, Li'l Bro. Do ya think the witch would approve? Givin' me money to fix a hog?"

"Jenny?"

"Ya, Jenny."

"We wouldn't need to tell her."

"Come on kid, you know better. Tell me you got the dough under your mattress."

Danny bites his lip. He has moved the eagle jacket to under his mattress, laid out smooth so it won't wrinkle. "What about Mom? She's got money."

GW moans so loudly that Danny holds the phone away from his ear. Bobbie chatters in the background.

"Don't go there, Li'l Bro. Mom's busy with her computers. She's even asked me for money."

"I need to go real bad," Danny sobs. "Need to get away from here."

"Know the feeling, Li'l Bro. Gets on your nerves, always havin' people tell'n ya what ta do."

Danny bites his knuckle. Tears well up behind his eyeballs. At Hamm, he'd have kicked the wall, but not here with Mr. Nowell watching.

"So sorry, Li'l Bro. It ain't gonna work." There's a long pause. "Ya wanna talk to Bobbie?"

"Naw." He shudders. Bobbie has become his nightmare, she's taken away his family. *GW ain't there for me, no more.*

"Sure?"

"Sure."

"Talk to you later."

Danny clutches the phone and listens as GW clicks off. The dial tone rings in his ears. He heads to his room and lies on his bed.

If I found money
If GW could fix his hog
We'd be family again

Get me hog fix'ins
Keep a dreamin' of Sturgis
Find money fast

WAITIN' FOR MONEY

"MONEY, MONEY, MONEY." Walter, Anne and Danny shout as a meteor streaks across the twilight sky. They sit by a fire at the Goulette lodge. A train's whistle echoes across the river. A high-flying airplane on route from Minneapolis to Chicago interrupts the sex songs of the frogs and crickets.

"Read your letter in the newspaper," Mr. Goulette says. "Good job."

"Ya think so?"

"You bet." Mr. Goulette sips cinnamon coffee and stretches his long legs to warm the bottom of his Red Wing boots. A fuzzy feeling creeps through Danny's body, a pleased feeling that Mr. Goulette would read his letter. He has a dream that his dad read the letter, too. In the dream, his dad takes Danny back home to his grandma's house. They all sit around the table, his mom, his dad, and GW, drinking coffee and eating donuts. Even Bobbie is there.

A second train whistles. Mr. Goulette tosses a log on the fire.

"I'm proud of you, too." Anne says. "Takes guts to stand up for what you think. The beavers and the muskrats have enough trouble raising babies and keeping safe. It's so sad, very sad." She enunciates 'sad' like an actress reading Shakespeare.

"Remember, it's called progress," teases Mr. Goulette. He

tosses a second log in the fire. Sparks swirl up as if they are lightning bugs caught in a chimney thermo.

"Can I join the C-CAPS? I'd like to do something," Anne says.

"Me, too," Mr. Goulette says. "Can't make the meetings, but I can give money."

Money. Danny takes a deep breath. *I need money, money for an adventure. Nowells called the riverboat an adventure, didn't tell Jenny that I'd run away. This time, I'll make the adventure Sturgis.*

"You want to come with? The C-CAPS meets tomorrow. Mr. Nowell and me can pick you up."

Anne nods. Danny settles back into his thoughts as he watches the fire burn. *She'll have a hundred dollars. Maybe I can write another letter for C-CAPS asking for money. Send the checks to me. No, what did Mr. Nowell say? Ask the reader to do what you want. Ask for cash. Send a hundred dollars to Danny Malloy, Samurai and help save the river.* He smiles. If he's learned one thing living at Nowells, it's to have a strategy. *I need Sturgis, and Sturgis needs money.*

> *Think it out today*
> *Make plans to send me money*
> *Be Samurai smart*

Good News-Bad News

Jeff begins the C-CAPS meeting, "We've got good news tonight." He waves a sheaf of papers high over his head. "Listen to this! Headlines in the <u>Saint Paul Pioneer Press</u> read: Lake Pepin power plan generates little support. Does it make sense to use 667 megawatts of electricity to generate 500 megawatts?"

"No!" Shouts shimmer the tin ceiling. The room buzzes with new people, including Anne. The guy from Rochester sits with two friends. Mrs. Crow has brought her boater friends. She's wearing a Honolulu dress and canvas shoes. Danny counts sixteen people. The Norwegian isn't there.

"Here's a letter from IWLA, the Isaac Walton League," reads Jeff. "They say the pump storage is extremely damaging to the environment, would increase air pollution, is not needed by our area, and would destroy an area of tremendous scenic and recreation value."

"Hooray!" Everyone in the room shouts again. Danny watches the tin ceiling tiles shimmer again. The Honeydos clap a high five. Mr. Nowell stomps his feet and whistles through his teeth. The Cookie Lady wipes her eyes.

"There's more," Jeff says. "People with real know-how are writing letters concerned about the reservoir being located on Karst, carbonated bedrock. The reservoir would cause conditions to induce sinkholes. Karst might make the bluffs act like a sieve causing water to drain through the bluffs. Remember the car wash?"

The crowd laughs.

"Here, Here!" He holds up more pages. "This letter says exposure to a large electromagnetic field induced by high voltage transmission lines poses health risks to humans, livestock, and wildlife. I guess the power company plans to string a transmission line across the river to Wisconsin." *And, to my dragon,* Danny moogles.

"And there's more." Jeff talks fast and loud. "People write there is a need for studies related to fish entrainment and mortality. What happens when at its lowest flow rates, the river's flow is exceeded by the rate of pumping water uphill to the reservoir? Would the river flow upstream?"

The words make Danny's head spin.

Jeff continues, "Another writer is concerned about the dewatering of springs caused by locating a power station in a single underground cavern below lake level. These experts wonder how the pumped storage project will affect silting in the river channel below Lake Pepin."

Mr. Nowell jumps up. He pumps his arms up and down in quick jerks as if he's lifting weights, and he stomps his feet.

"There's a ton more," Jeff says, breathlessly. "Seems the company hired to do the research, also plans to make a bid to manage it." Jeff holds up another letter. "This writer says the project needs an independent review."*

One of the boaters gives a cat call and everyone claps.

"All these letters mean we got help."

The group cheers. The Honeydos stand up and clap together another high-five. Mr. Nowell takes out his hanky and wipes his forehead. Then the meeting is over.

Anne gives Mr. Nowell the envelope from her dad. He waves her off to Jeff, who puts the money in his pocket. Danny watches.

"Guess you won't have to write anymore letters," Jeff says,

approaching Danny. "But you wrote a good one. People got stirred up!"

"I did?"

"You did."

Danny takes Anne's hand and leads her to the cookies. "Take two," he says, reaching for the chocolate chip circles. On the ride back to the Nowells, he moogles:

Up side and down side
Find another way to get
To my hog heaven
*See author's notes.

TURTLE TIME

DANNY COMES INTO the Goulette lodge "grinning and spinning" after doing morning barn chores and eating a pile of pancakes with raspberry syrup. He gives a war hoop, hugs Charlie and waits for the dog's ever loving, wet, slurpy kisses. Anne and Walter sit at the picnic table with what's left of their morning's breakfast. Danny grabs a piece of cold toast and spreads it with crunchy peanut butter.

"Its baby turtle time," Anne announces.

"Turtle time?" *Oh no!* "Why can't the old mothers just lay their eggs at McCarthy Lake?" He wipes his mouth on his blue shirt sleeve. He pours himself a cup of coffee and adds milk and sugar to the brim.

"Baby turtles need us," Anne says, "and we need to go back. You know what happens to turtles on the road?" She gives him her look that says *'stupid'.*

He stares back. *'Bossy'!*

"Should have gone out for football," Walter smirks. He punches Danny's shoulder. Walter has been getting in shape for football, while Danny has been mowing lawn, weeding, and getting bitten by chiggers. Mrs. Nowell's garden has a nest of chiggers. She put a piece of black paper on the ground and told Danny to watch. He saw a hundred or so of the little buggers. The little red creatures somehow crawl under his belt and make welts on his belly that itch like crazy. To stop the itch, Mrs. Nowell painted her fingernail polish on each bite. "Smothers the eggs," she said.

"If it's nice, we'll go on a turtle mission tomorrow," Anne says.

Danny shakes his head and groans. He wants to say *'no'.* *It's not just the baby turtles, but Sky Star's grave, and maybe seeing VanOort. But, if I stay home, Mrs. Nowell will have more weeds and more chiggers.*

"Should have gone out for football," Walter says again.

If he only knew, I could scare away any football team with my belly. Mrs. Nowell had painted his chigger bites with red nail polish.

"So, if Anne and me do turtles tomorrow, let's you and me go biking today," Danny says.

"Snake Creek Valley?" Walter asks.

"Spinning and grinning, okay, but no fishin'," Danny says.

Anne puts her hands on her hips. "What about me?"

BABY TURTLES

DANNY AND ANNE bring their bikes to a stop on CR 84 near the rare turtle and Weaver Dune signs. The early afternoon heat shimmers above the tarvy. Anne wears white tennis shoes and a red cotton shirt tucked in her blue jeans. Danny wears a cap, a matching Twins tee, and his old jeans.

Danny pants to catch his breath. *Wonder if she's brought water.* He doesn't ask.

"Baby turtles are the size of quarters," Anne says. She holds up her hand and touches her thumb and middle finger.

Why couldn't the old mommas just dump their eggs at McCarthy Lake? Because they're females and females cause trouble, he answers himself. *If they didn't cross the road, I wouldn't be here sweatin' in the hot sun. There'd never been a Sky Star, a dead woman, or a VanOort remindin' me I'm a JD, a foster kid, and makin' me feel bad, bad.*

A car roars in the distance. They watch it approach lickety split and step off the soft blacktop onto the gravel shoulder. The driver blasts his horn as if they can't see him.

"Thank goodness, no babies," Anne says, scanning the road ahead. "But look." A green and brown van crawls out of the Weaver dunes. "We've seen that one before."

"Oh, no," Danny mutters, "The Norwegian."

The truck's gears grind as the driver down shifts and rumbles southward toward Schmoker's Bridge. The truck backfires as it picks up speed.

"Must be in a hurry." Anne leans her bike on the 'rare turtle' sign and walks toward the tire tracks. She motions Danny to follow. "Come, let's look. The dunes aren't sacred."

Danny folds his arms across his chest. He grunts like Mr. Nowell. The tire tracks weave a trail between weeds, sand burrs, cockleburs and grasses, a large quilt of colors dotted with bushes and trees.

"Come on!" Anne waves him forward.

"Don't wanna," he protests.

"Why not? Are you a scared-ee cat?"

"I'm not scared, but—" *But why the Norwegian? Why'd he leave Snake Creek? Besides, the guy eats Nut Goodies, has a gun and a coyote-dog, who may be a ghost or a changeling.*

"Come, I want to see this," she calls. She trudges over a dune and disappears.

Danny sighs, heads in her direction and plods over a ridge thirty-feet high. He sees Anne chase a butterfly. He sits down and empties sand from his tennis shoes.

"Hey, Anne!" he yells, "what about the turtles?"

WEAVER DUNES

"POISON TO YOU and me," Anne tells Danny when he catches up. A butterfly flutters over a stalk of brown. "It's a sand milkweed. The butterflies love it."

"Oh!"

Another butterfly hovers nearby.

"Look," she motions him on. "Cliff goldenrod, Blue stems, Turkey feet." She points to the stalk of three toes that really do look like a bird's foot. She's excited.

"I'm hot!" Danny lifts his tee to fan his chest. He looks for a shade tree.

"What's that on your belly?"

"Nothing." He pulls down his shirt. *"Nosy."*

"Something!" She steps closer and pulls up his shirt. "You're all red."

"I know, Mrs. Nowell."

"What'd she do to you?" Anne frowns, her eyes grow bright and she tugs on his shirt.

"Nothing." Danny tells about the chiggers.

"Ask her for clear polish the next time." Anne puts her hands on her hips. "From now on, I'm going to call you Red Belly, it's your Indian name."

A butterfly flits by and Anne chases it, calling over her

shoulder. "It may be a regal fritillary or an Ottoe skipper. They're rare and breed here in the dunes."

Danny follows. Over the next dune, he sees a garbage pit: refrigerators and stoves with the doors hanging open, a truck without tires, metal wire, old boards and a tent. Next to the tent, there's a campfire ring, a table and a chair, and a stack of wood, all within throwing distance of the rubbish. A spade is planted next to the fire ring like a flag pole. Danny walks closer and sees the green paint on the handle.

"It was a monarch," Anne says, catching her breath as she runs to him. She eyes the spade and looks at the green spot. "The shovel?"

"Spade," Danny growls, "Mr. Nowell's spade."

"What?"

"The spade. See the green paint." He points. Angry, fearful thoughts crash inside his head. He feels out of breath. "The Norwegian threaten us about messin' round his camp, and now, that's what we're doin'. Let's get out of here."

Anne frowns.

"When I saw him at Snake Creek he was friendly," Danny says, "but he has a gun. Said he was huntin' squirrels. But I don't know—"

"What don't you know," Anne asks.

"There's Mr. Nowell's spade, and this guy eats Nut Goodies. VanOort picked up Nut Goodie wrappers at Sky Star's grave."

"Are you sure?" She gives him her '*you're stupid*' stare.

"Just cause I've got red spots on my belly, I'm not stupid. We gotta get out of here." He grabs her arm, but she balks and plants her feet mule-like.

"Take the shovel," she demands. "It don't belong here."

"But what do I tell Mr. Nowell? He'll want to know where we found it, and then there'll be trouble."

"So? VanOort will want to know too."

"VanOort?" Danny gulps. His belly rumbles. *No. No. Not VanOort.*

Anne looks around and shields her eyes against the sun as if she's wearing a Twins cap. "This is a crazy place to live. The guy must be hiding." She points to the old refrigerators. "Who'd live by a dump? He must be bad, very bad."

"Bad?"

Anne gives him another *'you're stupid'* stare. Danny stares back.

"Bad is bad," she says.

> *Bad, bad hide away*
> *How many times has it been said*
> *JD is bad, bad*

"What's bad? What makes you think you're good?" He folds his arms over his chest. "Maybe he's hiding. I've hid lots of times. I hide when I'm running." He brushes away a tear on his cheek. Anne looks surprised.

"What are you saying?"

"You make everything you say as if it's the only way."

"Huh?"

"The Norwegian just doesn't want us nosing around. Maybe he found the spade. Maybe his camping permit ran out. Maybe he doesn't have the money to rent a room. Maybe he likes it here!"

"You're crazy."

"No, I'm not. When I'm on a run, I stay lots of places, in boxes and garbage cans. And I'm not crazy, scared, maybe. When I had trouble borrowing things, nobody cared. Now I have to live in a foster home." He stretches his arms to the sky.

Anne sits down, crossing her legs in front of her. She kicks off her shoes.

Suddenly, the whole summer zings before Danny: his mother's move, GW's trip to Sturgis, how he liked Bobbie and now he doesn't, how the Indians got moved out of Snake Creek Valley to Crow River, how the government let Reads Landing get flooded, how the Blandings almost lost McCarthy Lake, and how every time he turns around there's VanOort.

"It's your fault, you and your damn turtles," he sobs. *If I was home, I'd walk out the door and slam it real hard. Instead, here I am, beside a garbage dump.* "You ratted on me to VanOort. I shoud'a run when my mom moved. Everythin' happenin' is bad." He sniffs and wipes his nose on his tee, carefully, so Anne can't see his belly.

Anne pats the ground, inviting him to sit. "Maybe it's not just you. I'm bad, too. I took my aunt's cigarettes so you could have smoke sticks. And, I'm a half-breed. Some kids call me apple, red on the outside but white inside. Sometimes I feel American and sometimes Indian, but I never feel all Dakota. I want to make a Jingle dress and dance at the powwow next summer. The Jingle Dance is a dance of healing, but I'm scared. I don't know how to do the dance, and I need a Jingle Dance dress. What if no one helps me?" She hiccups. "I wish I had some water."

A Norwegian Tale

"There's water in the cooler," a man's voice says, quietly. A wet nose kisses Danny's ear, then a dog's tongue swipes his cheek. He reaches for the coyote-dog and hugs its neck.

"You live here?" Anne slips her shoes back on.

"Guess so," the Norwegian answers. He opens the cooler and pulls out three bottles. He's wearing boots with thick soles and his dark glasses.

"Why'd you move from Snake Creek?" Danny asks.

"'Cause." The Norwegian gives them each a bottle of water. "The nature of my beast, I guess. Just can't stay too long in one place, always been on the move." He sits on his the camp chair.

"Once, I had a house and kid like you, been years since I've seen him." The Norwegian looks at Danny hard. "How old are you?"

"Fourteen, goin' on fifteen."

The man nods. "I guess that's about right."

"You've got a family?" Anne asks.

"Had, I guess, ran away, mostly from me. Couldn't take the wife naggin', the bills, the groceries and hearin' the kid cry. Just too much."

"And you live here, now," Anne asks.

"Not for long, I'm movin' on. Fall's a comin."

"Where will you go?" Anne asks.

"Don't know. Where my spirit leads me."

"Will you go back home?"

"Naw, the kid's better off without me. He's got a good ma."

Danny swallows some water. *This could be my dad talkin'.* He remembers hearing his mom and dad fight. Money. Bills. GW in trouble, then his own trouble with the teachers and borrowin' stuff. *What was it GW said about their dad? He ran away from himself.*

"So, why'd you come here?" Anne asks.

"Long story." The Norwegian looks at Danny. "You a foster kid?"

Danny nods.

"So was I, when I wasn't runnin'. Spent a year here in Snake Creek Valley. Best time of my life. And the old lady, who died back in the woods, was my neighbor. Closest thing to an angel, ever. Good to me. Baked me cookies. Hired me to clean her barn. Gave me honest pay and respect. In fact, the day she died, I met her there in the woods and she gave me all the money in her purse. Wanted me to have it. Told me to go home and see my kid. I took the money, planned to send it to my wife. Then I heard you kids."

"And," Anne says.

"Guess I got scared. You burying the turtle. Mrs. Chester sittin' there by the tree. Didn't know she'd died, till you found her."

Anne frowns.

"Who'd believe I didn't rob her? Her husband never did like me. Said 'cause I was a foster kid, I must be bad."

Danny quivers. A butterfly flutters through the camp site and lands on a stalk of blue stem.

"Mrs. Chester was like your Nowell." The Norwegian looks at Danny, pauses, and tips his water bottle to his lips and swallows. "Some people have a bigger picture of life than just themselves. Nowell worries about the river and it looks like he takes good care of you. Gives you respect. Seems to me, he treats everybody with respect, like Mrs. Chester. She loved the river and loved living here at Snake Creek. I guess I stayed the summer for her, gave C-CAPS some of her money."

The Norwegian drinks more water, then heaves the bottle into the pit. A scrambling noise comes from one old refrigerator.

"Rat," the Norwegian says. The dog jumps up, approaches the old refrigerator, barks and wags its tail.

"Let it be," the man yells to the dog. "When I was young like you, living here at Snake Creek, I never should have run away."

Gotta Go

"We gotta go," Anne pokes Danny's ribs. She gives him a stare then looks at the spade.

"Not yet," Danny says. "There's more."

Anne frowns.

"We gotta tell him about the sheriff."

Anne gives him her stare.

"No, it's only fair." Danny looks at the Norwegian.

"We gotta tell ya. After we buried Sky Star, the turtle, Anne had to give it a name 'cause she's Indian, she went and got the sheriff. Then, the sheriff came and got me and Mr. Nowell. Asked me all kinds of questions, mostly let me know, he don't like foster kids."

The Norwegian nods. "Been there, same song, different sheriff."

"Brought me back to the turtle grave and picked up stuff. The next morning, Anne and me look for the purse and the spade, and see boot prints on the turtle's grave. Weren't mine, so Anne says we have to go and tell the sheriff. This time he comes, and his deputy digs up the grave. She finds the purse with the money gone."

The Norwegian nods.

"So the sheriff thinks the lady's been robbed. She'd been paid a couple of hundred dollars her husband said. VanOort thinks I stole the purse."

The Norwegian nods again.

"So, the sheriff sent the evidence off to the state."

"Oh, I see." The Norwegian leans back in his chair, crosses his arms over his chest and rocks.

"So why'd you bury the purse," Anne asks.

"Guess I didn't think anyone would dig up the turtle grave. Nobody'd believe she gave me the money. It's an old feel'n you learn to live with."

"Bad is bad," Danny adds.

"Guess it comes with runnin'," the Norwegian says. "Feeling guilty even when you're not."

Anne stretches her arms toward the dog. The dog whines, and sits besides her. She pets its neck and strokes its back. The dog licks her cheek.

The Norwegian leans forward in his camp chair, resting his elbows on his knees. "So, what are you going to do? Tell the sheriff you found the spade and you know who's got her money?"

Anne stops petting the dog.

Danny takes a deep breath, a Samurai moment. *What is happening? What do I want to happen? How can I make it so?" This guy's an ant.*

"You know, I wrote a letter to the paper."

"Ya," the Norwegian says, "read it."

"I wrote the letter 'cause I didn't want the beavers, the muskrats and the birds to die, but I wrote it for another reason, my dad."

Both the Norwegian and Anne look at him.

"My dad ran away. My brother says he ran away from himself, like you. My house weren't the best place to be, but I miss him." Danny sniffs and wipes his nose on his tee. "I wrote the letter hoping he'd see it and be proud of me. I'm always hoping he'll find me. I guess I'm lookin' for a home and I'd like a dad. I bet your kid wants a dad, too. But it's not up to me, not up to Anne, just up to you."

"You're quite a kid," the Norwegian says. "Think the Nowell spirit has got you." He takes off his shades and rubs his eyes.

"We'll be back tomorrow to get the spade," Danny says. He takes Anne's hand. "I'll ask Mr. Nowell to come with, he'll know what to do."

"Okay," the Norwegian nods. "Just a minute before you go." He walks into the tent, and returns with a knapsack. "Dog dragged it home." He hands the knapsack to Danny, then, he holds up a mask that looks old, like an ancient warrior. "I use the mask to scare guys away from my glory hole." He hands the mask and a black dog leash to Danny. "Take Dog with you. Keep him tied for a day or two. Feed him well. He likes to chase squirrels. Don't let him run away."

"Does he have a name," Anne asks.

"I call him Dog."

DOG WAYS

"WHAT ARE YOU going to do?" Anne looks at Danny and then at Dog, who sits alert, chewing his leash. Dog looks up with bright, eager eyes and wags his tail. He left the camp eager to go, prancing through the dunes on his leash as if he was the star in a parade. The dunes glow in the setting sun, brush and sand changing to muted shades of maroon. The late afternoon air is warm.

Danny lifts his bike from the roadside.

"How do you plan to get him home, Red Belly? It is a he?" She pulls the dog to his feet, checks his plumbing and hands the leash to Danny.

"Huh?"

"What are your options?" She looks at Danny with her *'you're so stupid'* stare. "You took the dog, now, what are you going to do?"

"Let him go. See if he follows." Danny straddles his bike seat.

"He'll go back to the camp," Anne says. "You know the Norwegian won't stay there." Dog whines.

"He don't fit in my basket," Danny says.

"Not in one piece," Anne laughs. "You'd have to cut off his legs or something."

"I don't have a knife."

"If we can't ride our bikes, we'll walk home."

"Ya, fifteen miles or so?"

"Well, you're the master of running away. Can't you do fifteen miles, Red Belly?"

"And leave my bike?" Danny pats the bike's handlebars and shakes his head.

"We can just sit here and wait till someone misses us."

"Like who?"

"VanOort!" Anne giggles.

"I don't think you're funny," Danny grumbles. "It'd be VanOort all right. He shows up all the time, every place I go to see if I'm spending the old lady's money, because of you." He folds the mask into the knapsack and puts it all in Anne's basket.

"Sorry, Danny, but it was the right thing to do. Anyway, we've got a new problem, a live dog."

Dog jumps on Anne and nuzzles his nose into her shirt pocket.

"Sorry, no treats. No food and no water." She pushes the dog down and pats his nose. "Good boy."

"Well, maybe he'll run beside us, if we go slow." Danny balances the bike between his knees, and lifts the leash so the dog stands. He moves the bike forward, touching the road with the toes of his Nikes. Dog moves with him.

"How long do you think this will take?" Anne asks as she pedals her bike in circles along side him.

"Till dark, I s'pose."

They move beyond the rare turtle sign and the sign that welcomes visitors to the Weaver Dunes.

Dog winds the leash around his nose, prances, and at times, pulls Danny off balance.

"Let me take him." Anne reaches for the leash and Dog lunges free. He heads across the road and into the dunes.

"Let him go." Danny shakes his hands and braces his bike, feet flat on the road.

"We can't let him go, not with the leash. He'll get caught on a tree or a bush and hang himself."

Danny moans, puts down his bike, and follows the dog back into the dunes. *Why does this feel like a turtle mission? I hope we don't find a dead lady.*

Ahead, over a rise of dune, the dog chases a bird into a field of tan-colored balls the size of soccer balls.

"Yikes."

"Sand Prairie melons," Anne says, catching up from behind him. "They're the best ever."

A bird flits up, circles and lands down field.

"They know a good thing," Anne laughs. "Even the deer. Look." She points to deer tracks and picks up a half-eaten melon. The golden insides drip with juice. Dog jumps up to grab it. Anne pulls her hand away and Dog settles for a piece left on the ground. He noses it, kneels on his front legs with his butt to the wind, and wags his tail.

"A melon-eating dog," Danny says.

"He's got good taste." Anne snickers. She wipes the palms of her hands on her jean legs.

"Gottcha!" Danny says and grabs the leash. Dog continues to eat. Danny jerks the leash and the dog resists leaving the melon.

"Maybe whoever owns this field will give us a ride to Kellogg," Anne says. "If we can get to Curly's Bait Shop, we can call Nowells."

BARGAIN

"CAN I KEEP him?" Dog lies under a kitchen chair, ears alert, his nose resting on his front paws.

Mrs. Nowell smiles at Danny and gives her husband a long look.

"We'll see," Mr. Nowell says. "Before I make any promises, I want to go out to the Dunes. You say the Norwegian guy has a camp next to a garbage pit? And he's got my spade, anyways, a spade with green paint?"

Danny nods.

"But first, I'll call the sheriff. Not good to meander into something that might be trouble."

In the morning, the sheriff waits by the Weaver Dune sign. Mr. Nowell stops, turns off the ignition and pulls on the brake. Danny and Anne tumble out of the truck and wave to Deputy Abbie Mae. She returns a wave and calls out, "Good morning." The sheriff and Mr. Nowell shake hands.

Anne leads the way. The dunes spread before them on a green and brown, grassy and weedy quilt, accented with red and yellow splotches. Butterflies flutter around the tall stalks of goldenrod. A bird streaks across the horizon faster than Danny can blink three times.

"Peregrine Falcon," Mr. Nowell says, "very fast bird. Once

threatened, but coming back. There are a couple of nests along the river." He smiles and lifts his arms to the sky. "This is a great place, falcons, butterflies, flowers, and melons, Sand Prairie melons. Melons like sand." The man pauses and looks at Danny. "Melons were once a huge cash crop along the river."

"He's gone," VanOort calls. "The tent's gone." All that remains is the spade and the garbage pit. Deputy Abbie Mae puts on gloves, pulls up the spade and puts it in a black, plastic bag.

"We'll check out the prints," she says to Mr. Nowell.

VanOort hunches down by the campfire ashes and stirs them with a stalk of turkey foot. He picks up the wrapper from a Nut Goodie candy bar.

"So, tell me what the Norwegian said." He shifts his weight on his haunches and looks at Anne.

Anne tells her story. Danny swallows hard when tempted to interrupt with questions he'd ask. *Will they arrest him? Will they put him in jail? Will his kid ever see his dad again?* Mr. Nowell rests his arm across Danny's shoulders.

"Well, we'll check it out," VanOort says.

"Look's like we need to check out the garbage, too," Mr. Nowell says. "Not good having people visit the dunes and see what the early farmers left. Not too long ago, everyone had a garbage pit in their back yard. Looks like this belonged to a nearby farm. I'll get a gang together and we'll clean it out. Something always needs doing along the river."

VanOort leads the way back through the dunes to CR 84. Abbie Mae drags the plastic bag. They walk past the field of soccer-ball melons. Mr. Nowell stops and points into the sun towards a second patch.

"Watermelons," he whispers. "We stopped there often when we camped at West Newton."

"You mean you borrowed 'em?"

"Don't tell the sheriff."

Danny chuckles and waves him off.

"In September," Mr. Nowell says, "we'll go to the Watermelon

Festival. Been going on in Kellogg for fifty years. There's a parade, and all the watermelon you can eat. Maybe you can ride Yago."

Back on CR 84, Deputy Abbie Mae puts the bag in the sheriff's trunk.

"Let me know when you plan to clean the site," VanOort says and shakes Mr. Nowell's hand. "Hope you don't find any dead bodies." The sheriff winks at Anne.

"Sure will," Mr. Nowell says, "got good help. Danny owes me."

"Owes you? Owes you for what," Danny challenges, as he climbs in the truck and makes room for Anne.

"For Dog. What will you pay me to keep Dog? Dogs costs money—vet bills and food. We'll have to make some new rules, feeding times, picking up poop, dog stuff." Mr. Nowell starts the engine, releases the brake and shifts gears.

"Crazy!" *Ain't anything ever free at the Nowells?* Danny braces his feet against the floorboard. "How about a blue-velvet eagle jacket, and seven dollars?"

"Sounds like a deal. Let's go home."

Author's Note

The Mississippi Valley Pumped-Storage Project was proposed in 1992 by the Southern Minnesota Municipal Power Agency (SMMPA) in a public hearing June 15, 1992 at the Lake City Minnesota High School. The concept of the project was to pump water from a lower reservoir (Lake Pepin) to an upper reservoir during periods of low electrical demand and then release the water during periods of high electrical demand. In November, 1990 SMMPA obtained a Preliminary Permit from the Federal Energy Regulatory Commission (FERC) to maintain priority as developer of the site. The proposed site was five miles southeast of Lake City and would include a 185-acre upper reservoir, a 2,100-foot water conductor system, a power station housing two 250-MW generating/pumping units, an existing lower reservoir, a switchyard and a tie line to an existing transmission line and access roads and tunnels.

On September 11, 1992, SMMPA announced it had dropped from participation a study of the feasibility of constructing the Mississippi Valley Pumped-Storage Project. More information on this project can be found by requesting the FERC Project file #10941, minutes of SMMPA's Board of Directors Meeting and a news release, Sept. 11, 1992. More information is also available from the following Minnesota area newspapers: St. Paul Pioneer Press, Minneapolis Star Tribune, Wabasha Herald, and the Rochester Post Bulletin, from June to September, 1992.